"My life's purpose is here," Claire said.

"What is it?" Reed asked. "Your life's purpose?" He couldn't help himself. Did he have one of those?

Claire's face brightened. "I've always been the one my brothers and sisters lean on for support. I didn't fully appreciate it until I left." She shrugged. "Besides, I've said it before, I want a man to put me first."

"What category would you put me in?"

A genuine smile spread across her face. "Not selfish. Not one bit. You've done so much to help our town. We're all grateful. I'm grateful."

"But?"

Claire glanced a̶̶̶̶̶̶̶̶̶̶̶̶̶̶̶̶̶̶̶̶̶̶̶̶̶̶̶̶̶̶̶̶̶̶̶̶̶ her face. "But it's tak̶̶̶̶̶̶̶̶̶̶̶̶̶̶̶̶̶̶̶̶̶̶̶̶̶̶̶̶̶ zoo to become av̶̶̶̶̶̶̶̶̶̶̶̶̶̶̶̶̶̶̶̶̶̶̶̶̶̶̶̶̶̶̶̶̶̶̶ the otters every d̶̶̶̶̶̶̶̶̶̶̶̶̶̶̶̶̶̶̶̶̶̶̶̶̶̶̶̶̶̶̶̶̶̶̶

He nodded, his heart strangely heavy. Everything she said was true. Her honesty pressed against his chest, though. Made him want to reveal more. "I'm leaving because I'm good at my job. I'm not good at the other stuff."

"What other stuff?"

"Getting close."

"Why do you say that?" she asked.

He stared at the tree line. There was so much about him she didn't know.

Jill Kemerer writes novels with love, humor and faith. Besides spoiling her mini dachshund and keeping up with her busy kids, Jill reads stacks of books, lives for her morning coffee and gushes over fluffy animals. She resides in Ohio with her husband and two children. Jill loves connecting with readers, so please visit her website, jillkemerer.com, or contact her at PO Box 2802, Whitehouse, OH 43571.

Books by Jill Kemerer

Love Inspired

Small-Town Bachelor

Visit the Author Profile page at Harlequin.com for more titles

Small-Town Bachelor

Jill Kemerer

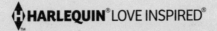

HARLEQUIN® LOVE INSPIRED®

Recycling programs
for this product may
not exist in your area.

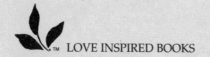

LOVE INSPIRED BOOKS

ISBN-13: 978-0-373-87953-3

Small-Town Bachelor

Copyright © 2015 by Jill Kemerer

www.Harlequin.com

Printed in U.S.A.

God sets the lonely in families,
He leads out the prisoners with singing;
but the rebellious live in a sun-scorched land.
—*Psalms* 68:6

To my husband, Scott. You're my champion, my encourager, my love. And to Mom, Dad and Sarah for a lifetime of love and support.

Chapter One

Weddings. Months of buildup, CIA levels of planning, and worth every second if it made her sister happy.

Claire Sheffield scraped a long silver ribbon over the edge of the scissors and admired the resulting curl. Rain splashed against the windows of Uncle Joe's Restaurant. Almost midnight and growing windy. Hopefully, the wedding wouldn't be plagued with bad weather tomorrow. Severe storms were common in southern Michigan, especially in mid-June. At least the reception would be here, indoors, where nothing could touch the bridal party. A slight shift in the air created a frenzy of flubbing noises in the corner where seventy-five more balloons waited to be tied into bunches.

White linens draped the tables, tall hurricane vases contained fresh pillars ready to be lit and party favors tucked in miniature silver boxes were swathed in pink ribbons. To round out the decor, blush-colored roses waited in the refrigerator.

Claire had decorated the rustic waterfront restaurant for family weddings twice before, though neither of her brothers' marriages had lasted. And what about her own disastrous try at love? Following Justin to another state had cost Claire the job of a lifetime. Here it was, five years later, and she finally had another chance to be a veterinarian technician at the zoo. She'd never throw away the opportunity again. Certainly not for a guy.

But this wedding wasn't about Claire. It was about her baby sister. Was Libby ready for marriage?

The door opened, letting in a blast of wind, rain and the best man...Reed Hamilton, looking as if he just stepped out of the shower.

Whoa! He was hot enough to melt the ice sculpture sitting on the second shelf of the walk-in freezer.

Reed ran his hand over his head, his cropped brown hair standing in little spikes as water dripped down the sides of his cheekbones to his square jaw. He had a natural ease about him, and the way he moved? Athletic. The scent of rain and woods trailed him inside. Sometime between the rehearsal dinner and now, he'd lost the tie, leaving his dress shirt open at the collar.

His tawny brown eyes held her gaze a touch too long before he cleared his throat. "The weather's getting bad. Libby was worried you wouldn't have a ride."

Reed was offering her a ride home?

Made sense, since he was staying next door in Granddad's empty cottage all weekend. "Thanks. Ten more minutes and I would have called one of my brothers."

Thunder cracked. She slapped her palm over her thumping chest. Was the sky turning a different color? Or did she imagine the olive tint to the darkness?

Reed shoved his hands in his pockets and perused the space. "How much do you have left to do here?"

"A few more bunches to hang."

"Let me help." He nodded to the table where she'd set spools of ribbons, tape, scissors, markers and various other essentials.

A ride home *and* an offer to help? Her brothers avoided

anything that involved decorating, which explained the bare walls and worn furniture in their house.

Lightning lit the sky, and the low wail of sirens commenced.

Sirens meant one thing.

Tornado.

The slender strings slipped through her fingers. Claire hurried down the ladder. "We have to find cover." Where was the safest place for them to go?

"Come on." Reed propelled her toward the door leading to the kitchen. "Is there a basement? A cellar?"

"No." The hair at the nape of her neck rose. She couldn't think of a worse place to face a tornado. Her eyes blinked uncontrollably until Reed pressed his hand against her lower back.

"Hey, it's going to be okay." His calm tone steadied her. "But we need to get out of this room."

"You're right." She raced ahead of him. "The staff bathroom—cement blocks and no windows. It's our best option."

She plunged through the hall, past the bank of ovens, the pantry and the walk-in refrigerator. Reed followed her into the large bathroom.

"Get on the floor—" But whatever he said next ripped from his mouth as the walls shook.

She fell to her knees. Hunched over. Tried to get as small as possible.

Please, God, protect us!

The wind screeched, shaking the structure as if it were a cardboard box. Her knees dug into the cold, hard tiles. Reed flung his arm over her shoulders, shielding her body with his.

"Cover your head," he yelled. The storm roared like a freight train.

Her teeth chattered, her arms shook and terror such

as she'd never known consumed her. A wrenching sound could only be the roof. *Lord, please, Lord, please...* Even with the protection of Reed's body, rain, sticks and stones pelted her. A tree groaned, toppling over them and crashing onto the far wall. Reed's muscles tensed as he rolled to the side. Her experience treating injured animals alerted her he'd been hurt.

"Reed?" she shouted. "Are you okay? Reed?"

He squeezed her arm—*praise the Lord!*

An eternity passed. Claire lay facedown on the floor while the chaos continued.

The commotion died to a thunderstorm. She didn't move, didn't dare to, but she needed to assess the situation. Dread and fear tangled in her chest. What would she find?

"Reed?" Her stomach heaved. *Keep it together, Claire.* She gulped in a deep breath. "How badly are you hurt?"

"My leg," he said, his voice strained.

"Which leg?"

He groaned.

"Shh...don't move. I'll try to get this branch off you. Sit still." Her calm tone didn't match the reckless tempo of her heartbeat.

"I'm okay...are you?" His voice grew faint. "...need to get you out of here. Not safe..."

"I'm fine." A flash of lightning froze the scene before her like an eerie photo. The top of the tree had demolished the door. She gaped at the view beyond it. Where was the hallway? Rubble, at least five feet high, piled beyond the bathroom. They couldn't get out if they tried. And the rain continued to fall.

The restaurant...the wedding...destroyed.

Her breathing came in quick bursts. She wasn't prepared for this. Her cell phone was in her purse—out in the dining area. No towels, no first aid kit, not even a flashlight.

She could make out shapes, but without light, she couldn't gauge how badly Reed was injured.

Wiping away the rain dripping into her eyes, she inhaled for three counts. She worked fifty hours a week as a vet tech, assessing injured animals. She could do this!

"Hold still." Claire focused on Reed. "I'm going to examine you. I know you're hurt, so promise me you won't move."

His right calf and ankle had swollen considerably—a broken leg, she guessed—but no bones protruded. She gathered branches and leaves into a mound near his foot.

"I'm going to lift your leg. Gently. Brace yourself." With both hands she held his calf, setting it on the makeshift pile. She crawled back, brushing debris out of her way, and sat on the floor with her back against the wall. Lifting Reed's head, she placed it on her legs.

"You don't have to—" he said, his voice taut.

"Save your strength." She tried to think of anything else she could do. He needed a doctor, X-rays and painkillers. If only she had her cell phone. Why hadn't she thought to grab it? Maybe Reed had his. Hope rose. "Do you have your cell phone?"

"The car." A spasm seized his body. Claire wanted to shake her fist at the sky.

How long would they be trapped? Was her family okay? The thought of losing any of her loved ones made her stomach roil. Oh! What about the otters? Her sweet rescue otter babies. The forecast called for rain, so she'd left the cellar doors open, but would they know to go down there? And did they have time?

The mounting worries quickened her pulse until her body threatened to explode with pent-up energy.

God, I'm giving this to You.

Her tension lowered a notch. She had to believe everyone survived, including the otters. Her loved ones surely took refuge, and the otter twins would continue to be healthy and happy until they moved to the zoo later this summer.

Reed shifted, a hiss escaping his lips. Right now she had to concentrate on him. She stroked his hair the way she used to stroke Libby's when she was sick.

He had saved her. By all rights, she should have been the one pinned under the tree. Or worse. If he had come ten minutes later, she would have had to survive this alone.

"Thank you," she whispered.

She would make this up to Reed. Somehow.

Reed blinked repeatedly. Where was he? A blurry white ceiling and fluorescent lights stung his eyes. *Beep.* What was that smell? Rubbing alcohol? Astringent? It burned his nose. *Beep.*

He attempted to sit, but the tubes in his arm forced him back into the pillow. A cast encased his right leg from his foot to his knee. A white sheet covered the rest of him.

Last night dashed back. From the drive to Lake Endwell for Jake and Libby's rehearsal dinner, to his late appearance at the restaurant to take Claire home.

Claire.

Medium height, almost-black hair skimming her shoulders, slim and pretty. Very pretty. She had unusual eyes— a ring of indigo surrounded the palest blue—and a sweet smile. The kind of smile a guy could let go to his head, if he was the type to consider having a wife and family. Which he wasn't. Not even close.

Claire had taken care of *him* for hours in the dark. She had a soothing way about her, had handled the disaster calmly and kept up a steady stream of chatter until her dad found them and called an ambulance.

If Reed had to be trapped half the night with a broken

leg *and* rain pouring through a gaping hole in the ceiling *and* a tree on top of him, he was glad he'd been with Claire.

He frowned. Why was he thinking about her in that way?

She lived in Lake Endwell. The one place he avoided. His dad, stepmother and half brother, Jake, lived here and were just fine without him in the picture. The three of them had moved to Lake Endwell after Reed graduated from high school, and this was the first time Reed had visited in years. Chicago provided a necessary two-hour buffer. Barrier? Whatever. It all added up to the same thing—he didn't fit with them. Or with families in general. He'd ruined two already.

Reed had no clue how to make a relationship—any relationship—last.

"You're awake." Barbara, his stepmother, paused in the doorway, her lips not quite committing to a tremulous smile. Her short black hair skimmed her chin, and she wore a dark green sweater set with her ever-present pearls. Dressed up even after a tornado. She strode to his side and poured water into a small plastic cup. "Sip some of this. You must be thirsty. Do you want me to hold it for you?"

He should have known she'd be here, trying to play Florence Nightingale with him. Why she continued to make an effort, he didn't know. It wasn't as though he deserved her kindness. He'd always been cordial, but he preferred to keep a distance. Didn't want her poking and prying and getting close. Better that way.

He reached for the cup, grimacing when his trembling fingers spilled it.

"Let me." She placed it against his lips.

He dutifully took a sip. "Thanks." It came out more a croak than a word. His neck stiffened trying to hold his head up. "Claire?"

"She has a black eye and a few nasty scratches."

His head sank into the pillow. Why a stranger—Claire, of all people—brought out his dormant protective side, he didn't know, but last night he hadn't liked the thought of her walking home in the rain, nor did he like the thought of her with a black eye now. "What about Jake? Is he all right?"

"He's fine too. Rode out the storm in Dale's basement with Libby. I'll go get your father." She patted his hand and left the room.

Jake was okay. *Thank You, God.* Reed loved the kid— not that a twenty-three-year-old could be called a kid. A twinge of guilt prodded. When Jake asked him to be the best man, Reed had considered turning down the offer. What kind of big brother was he?

"How are you?" Dad shuffled in with his hands in his pockets. He didn't sit, just stood there shifting from one foot to the other. He nodded to the cast. "Rough getup."

Tension crackled, and a fissure of cool air rushed over Reed's skin, raising the hair on his arms. "Yeah."

A knock at the door startled them. Staring at a clipboard, a doctor entered the room and strolled to the bed. "Ah, I see you're awake."

"I'll wait outside." The creases in Dad's forehead deepened.

"Wait, Dad, don't—" But he disappeared out the door. What had Reed expected? The man had made an art out of slipping away. Reed's fingernails cut into his palms.

"How are you feeling? Tell me your pain level on a scale of one to ten." The doctor pushed a button, raising Reed's bed to a seated position, and checked him over.

"Four, I guess. I'm more stiff than sore."

"Good. Good. How is your leg?"

"You tell me."

The doctor scanned his notes, making a clicking sound with his tongue. "Broken tib-fib. Snapped in two places—

the right tibia and fibula. We inserted a pin to hold the broken ends together, and we didn't have any complications. We'll be keeping a close eye on it with X-rays over the upcoming weeks, but I believe you'll make a full recovery."

Reed's face must have betrayed his shock, because the doctor lowered his clipboard. "It could have been much worse. You're fortunate you had someone there to elevate it and keep it stable all those hours."

Reed agreed. Without Claire's help, he would be in much worse shape.

"The cast." Reed dipped his chin to indicate his leg. "How long will I have to wear it?"

"Plan on a minimum of six weeks."

Six weeks?

"No other injuries?" Reed asked. "Only the broken—what did you call it?"

"Tib-fib. You broke your leg. We'll keep you here overnight. In the meantime, I want you to give some thought to how you're going to manage at home. Do you have anyone who can help you get around?"

"I'll be fine." He'd figure it out. People got around in casts all the time. It wouldn't be that big a deal.

But what about Alaska? In all the chaos, he'd forgotten his monthlong trip to the last American frontier. The timing had been perfect. Do his duty as best man in Jake's wedding, squeal the tires out of Lake Endwell Sunday morning and drive across the upper states until he reached Bellingham, Washington. From there, he'd hop on a ferry for whale watching and spend the rest of the month exploring Alaska. Give him time to breathe before tackling his duties as the new vice president of Rockbend Construction. Eight years of intense work and he'd finally been offered the VP title he coveted. Everything had fallen into place.

Until this.

He swallowed the copper taste of disappointment. Why

had God allowed this to happen? Jake's wedding ruined. A broken leg the day before Reed's Alaskan adventure.

What now? He couldn't return to Chicago. An image of the busy sidewalks he navigated seared into his mind—it was hard enough getting around the city on two legs, let alone on one. And he didn't have anyone in Chicago who could help.

He'd just have to change his daily routine and walk less, drive more.

The doctor pulled out a stool and wheeled next to the bed. "The tibia supports the body's weight. Avoid putting any pressure on the leg for several weeks. We'll start you in a wheelchair, check the X-rays and if it's healing, we'll okay crutches. You'll still have to stay off this leg, though. Don't plan on driving until the cast is off."

Wheelchair?

No driving?

As if that was going to happen. He wouldn't bother telling the doc he had no intention of following his instructions. A wheelchair would never work in his high-rise apartment.

A sound startled him. Barbara hovered in the doorway, raised her eyebrows and fingered her pearls. "Doctor, would it be okay for Reed to have some lunch? He hasn't eaten since yesterday."

"Of course." The doctor rose. "If you have any questions, I'll be in later to check on you. And tell the nurse if you're experiencing any pain."

He was experiencing pain all right—the giant pain in the rear this injury had forced on him.

"I'll tell the nurse you're ready for some food." Barbara hesitated. "Or would you like us to bring something? Roger and I will gladly go to the cafeteria."

Yeah, Dad would *gladly* go to the cafeteria to avoid spending time with him. And Barbara would flutter around

and make the atmosphere even more charged. If he could
go back to sleep and not wake up until his leg was func-
tioning…

"That's okay." Reed gave her a tight smile. "I'll eat
whatever the nurse brings."

"Are you sure? I can find something specific, maybe
lasagna? You still like Italian food, right? Or a sub sandwich? Ham, turkey, roast beef. Chips. A pop—"

Lord, help me out. A little patience? "I'm not very hungry. Anything is fine."

"You look like you're not feeling well. Is your leg hurting? I'll send your dad back in while I find a nurse." She
scurried out, leaving him alone, to his relief.

A minute later, Dad appeared, as uneasy as earlier. "Did
the…uh…doctor fill you in on—" he waved his hand at
Reed's leg "—everything?"

Reed nodded.

"He told us you would need some help. Uh…I would
offer you a room, but…"

Disappointment flooded him, but Reed didn't show it,
wouldn't let Dad see how much his dismissal still hurt.
Would they ever get past the strain in their relationship?
"I got it covered."

He brightened. "We weren't sure what to do. The split-
level would be hard to navigate in your…um…condition.
The wheelchair, you know."

The split-level would be hard to navigate, but Reed
didn't doubt the real reason his dad didn't want him
around. They hadn't been relaxed in each other's presence in over twenty years. The death of Reed's mother
still tore them apart.

"Like I said." Reed attempted to sit up. "Don't worry
about it."

Dad stood there, swaying slightly, as if he wanted to

say something. Finally, he turned to go. "I'd better go see what's keeping Barbara."

Yes. He'd better go to Barbara. He'd been pulling that move for as long as Reed could remember.

Alone once more, Reed closed his eyes. Maybe he could book a flight back home tomorrow. But what about his truck? He'd driven into Lake Endwell with all his gear for the trip.

"Knock, knock." Claire smiled from the doorway, interrupting his thoughts.

Reed grinned, waving her inside. She eased into the chair next to his bed. His smile faded at her swollen face, her bandaged hand and the scratches on her bare arms. "Does your eye hurt?"

"Not really." She lifted her hand wrapped in gauze. "A few scrapes. Nothing a little time won't mend. The bigger question is how are you doing?"

He longed to touch her cheek, to thank her for taking care of him all those hours while they waited for rescue, but caution prevented the words from spilling. This intrigue couldn't be explored. Not with her, the one with the enormous family. The one who lived here. No matter how careful he was or how hard he tried to understand family dynamics, he failed. Every time.

Best to keep things light. Reed pointed to his cast. "Like my new look? Admit it—you're jealous."

Her laugh tinkled, did something weird to his pulse. "Insanely jealous. Want me to sign it for you?" Claire scooted forward a few inches.

"Of course. I saved you a big spot. There. By my knee." He pointed to his leg. "Need a Sharpie?"

"Only if it's purple. I'm surprised you didn't go with a colored cast. Fluorescent pink would have made you the envy of all the girls."

His lips twitched. "If I had known I could choose a color, I would have."

"Maybe next time."

"There won't be a next time."

"Don't be so sure," she said. "You'll probably get a new cast in two or three weeks."

"What do you mean?" He shifted, flinching as his foot bumped the bed rail.

"Your leg will shrink, and this cast won't fit. Plus, the doctors check your progress often. Don't get too attached to your current one."

"And here I was going to name it. Way to ruin it for me. How do you know so much about this anyway?"

"I have three brothers. In and out of the hospital all the time growing up. I'm also a vet tech."

Her brothers had been at the rehearsal dinner. They seemed like fun guys. "What's a vet tech? Something with cats, dogs and computers?"

"Something like that, minus the computers. I'm a veterinary technician at a local clinic now."

"Is it temporary or something?"

Pink tinted her cheeks. "No, it's permanent, but ever since I can remember, I've wanted to work for the zoo. I've volunteered there for years. A position is opening up later this summer."

"Why don't you work there already?"

She averted her eyes. "I had a chance once. But I turned it down. I won't again." She picked at the edge of the gauze on her hand. "Jobs are hard to come by at our zoo. They don't have a large budget, and when they hire someone, the person tends to stay."

He shrugged. "Work for a different zoo, then."

Her blank stare bored into him for a solid three seconds. Why was she looking at him as if he'd turned green?

"What?" he asked. "What did I say?"

"There aren't any other zoos around here."

"So? Move."

"Nope." She brushed her hands together in a dismissive motion. "Did that once. Lost my dream job and my heart in one fell swoop. I'm staying here, in Lake Endwell, where I belong. But hey, I didn't come in here to bore you with my life story."

Boring? Claire? Not possible. There had to be more behind her tale. One he wanted to hear someday.

"What's next?" she asked. "I mean, what happens now with your leg and all?"

What was next? Dinner, a movie, a good-night kiss? What was it about her that mellowed him? Brought out his playful side?

Her mention of losing her heart must have jarred his brain. Talk about bad timing for getting the urge to flirt. Maybe the painkillers were messing with his head.

"I was supposed to be off to Alaska. Looks like I'm heading back to Chicago instead."

"Alaska?" Her voice rose on the last syllable. "Why?"

He sighed. It rankled—having to cancel the trip. "I always wanted to explore the wilderness. Get back to nature for a month. Ride the ferries. See whales. Fish."

"I'm sorry, Reed." She *did* look sorry. "Sounds like something you've been planning for a long time."

"Yeah. Well, what do you do?"

Neither spoke as muffled conversations of doctors and nurses in the hallway and beeping sounds filtered through the room. Then she perked up.

"You can stay here. We have wilderness—well, a lake anyway. And Granddad's cottage is handicap accessible. You can fish off the end of the dock."

He didn't mean to grimace, but staying in Lake Endwell? In close proximity to Dad and Barbara? "I'll take my chances in Chicago."

She scolded him with her stare. How did women do that? "You're going to be in a lot of pain. Do you have anyone who can take care of you?"

"I don't need anyone taking care of me."

"Men," she muttered. "Listen, there's no way the doctor is going to let you get on a plane for at least a week. You can ride it out in this noisy hospital room or relax in a beautiful cabin on the lake. Seems like an easy choice to me."

She had a point. He waved to his leg. "I can't sit around here forever."

"No one said anything about forever. Just until you get back on your feet. Literally."

He chuckled. Beautiful and funny? Killer combination.

Maybe staying in a cottage on the lake wasn't such a bad consolation prize. And why worry about being around Dad and Barbara? They would avoid him as usual.

Wouldn't they?

There was a chance—a slight chance—for him and Dad to work through their problems. If not, it didn't matter. Reed could spend more time with Jake. He missed him.

"Guess it wouldn't hurt." He shrugged. "It's not like they're expecting me at work."

"See?" She beamed. "There you go. What do you do anyway?"

"Commercial construction. Until yesterday, I was the senior project manager, but they're promoting me to vice president. I'll take over mid-July when the current VP retires."

"Wow!" Her whole face lit up. "Vice president. Congratulations. And you work in construction? Lake Endwell could sure use some help with that. I guess the town was hit pretty hard."

Main Street of Lake Endwell stuck in his head. The historic brick storefronts, bright red and navy awnings, flowers planted everywhere. Had the twister demolished the village? Would be a shame. He'd always had a soft spot for picturesque American towns. But helping them rebuild might give him something to do other than sitting around staring at his cast. "Did your house get damaged?"

"I don't think so. Trees are still blocking my road, but the reports sound good so far." Her chipper tone didn't mask the anxiety in her eyes. Tendrils from her ponytail wrapped around her neck. "If you stay for a while, we'll be neighbors, so I'll make sure you're fed. Wait—let me rephrase that—I'll bring over Aunt Sally's delicious food. You don't want me to cook."

He laughed but frowned inside. Was she this generous with everyone? This trusting? They'd only met a few hours ago, and she was already treating him like…one of the family.

"You don't even know me," Reed said.

"What are you talking about?" Her nose scrunched as she waved her hand. "You're Jake's brother. You're family."

His hunch was right. The fact that she'd tossed him into that category sobered him more than a bucket of ice water to the face.

"You're probably tired. I'll let you get some sleep." She covered his hand with hers. "Thanks again, for being there during the tornado, for protecting me."

He slid his hand out from under hers. "I didn't do much."

"Didn't do much?" she said. "I could have—"

"It was nothing." Too abrupt, his tone, but he couldn't help it.

"Whatever you say, Reed." And she padded out of the room.

Yes, if he was staying in Lake Endwell, he needed a powerful distraction from his pretty neighbor.

His experience with disaster relief provided the perfect excuse. There would be too much work for the local builders to complete by themselves. He'd make calls to find the best construction crews in the surrounding counties and help get the rebuilding efforts started. But as soon as the doctor cleared him, Reed was hightailing it back to Chicago.

Chapter Two

Exhaustion turned her legs to sandbags. As soon as she left Reed's room, Claire returned to the hospital's main waiting area and craned her neck to spot her dad. Assured Reed would be okay, she wanted nothing more than to go home and make sure the otters were safe. She'd go on foot if necessary.

"Oh, honey, you're fortunate you survived." Aunt Sally's bleach-blond hair bounced and her disco-ball earrings bobbed like fishing lures on the lake. "I don't know how either of you made it out without more severe injuries. Joe called. He said the restaurant is a wreck. The dining hall's intact, but the back rooms are destroyed. I'm so glad you're okay." She embraced Claire again. "You're going to fall over if you don't park it."

"Where's Dad?" Claire hugged her arms into her abdomen. "I've got to get home."

"I'll find him. You sit."

Claire collapsed in the chair. Her other family members clutched foam coffee cups and chatted in clusters, filling the space. To see Tommy, Bryan, Sam, Libby and everyone else alive and healthy after the awful night—it humbled her. *Thank You, Lord, for protecting everyone I love.*

"Your face looks terrible." Libby took the chair next to

Claire. Her long blond hair hadn't been brushed, and her eyes were red rimmed from crying. "Aren't you supposed to have this ice pack on it?"

"It's nothing. I'm more worried about you. How are you holding up?" Claire accepted the ice pack from Libby and pressed it to her cheek, flinching when the cold stung her bruise. "I'm sorry about the wedding. We'll get it all planned and perfect again."

"I'm just glad you're alive."

"Me too."

"When I think about the restaurant and everything ruined… We should be at the church right now." A stream of tears gushed down Libby's cheeks, and Claire pulled her close, rubbing her back. Jake came over and took Libby in his arms. Claire shot him a grateful smile, struck at the similarities between him and Reed. Both hovered around six feet tall and shared a muscular build. Libby took a tissue from Aunt Sally while Jake checked his watch.

"Man, I feel so bad for Reed." Jake sighed. "He gets into town and this happens. And he was supposed to leave for Alaska right after the wedding. Claire, thanks again for taking care of him."

"Don't feel bad. It wasn't your fault. And it was the least I could do after Reed saved my life. If he hadn't protected me, I would have been the one crushed under the tree. Or worse." She shuddered. "I think I have him talked into staying in Granddad's cottage until he's recovered a bit."

"Good idea! And thank the good Lord he showed up when he did." Aunt Sally clapped her hands to get the room's attention. "It's been a long night and an even longer morning. Why don't you all take a break at my house for a few hours? A lot of cake will go to waste if we don't start eating it."

"The wedding cake?" Libby paled. "I can't eat that! It's supposed to be—"

"It's food." Aunt Sally wrapped her arm around Libby. "We'll make another when you get a new wedding date."

Libby swallowed and nodded, walking with Sally to the door as the groups dispersed.

Tommy, Bryan and Sam approached Claire. "Come on, you can ride with us."

"Still no word on the otters?" She nibbled the corner of her lower lip. "Have you called Dad lately? Is the road clear?"

Tommy swiped his hand over his eyebrow. "The otters are fine—"

"How do you know?" Her voice rose. Maybe Tommy checked on them. "Did you get through?"

"No, but—"

"Don't patronize me, Tommy. I'm responsible for them until they move to the zoo. And I'm having a hard enough time thinking about them leaving next month. If they were hurt or worse—"

"Stop. I got it." Tommy extended his palms out in defense and widened his eyes at Bryan, who held a cell phone against his ear. "Well?"

Bryan slid the phone back into his pocket. "Didn't answer." He glanced at the elevator. "Oh, that's why."

Dad strode to them and patted Claire's shoulder. "The crews have most of your road clear, Claire-bear. Come on, I'll take you home."

Claire-bear. Dad must have been worried sick last night. He hadn't used his pet name for her in years.

"Thanks, Dad."

Ten minutes later, Dad drove the back roads to the lake. It was turning out to be a beautiful, sunny day, but branches and trees littered the ground. Half a mile from town, a partially destroyed building with a caved-in roof spilled insulation out the missing side wall.

Damaged roofs, pole barns stripped to their frames,

rubble-covered sidewalks, furniture strewn through the streets, cars flipped over in yards—everywhere Claire looked there was devastation.

"Whoa," she said. "Is it like this all over?"

Dad slowed to avoid a set of patio cushions. "One side of Main Street is unrecognizable. The twister took out several roofs in the new subdivision and ripped up trees on a warpath to the restaurant, but it curved away from there. That's what I'm being told, at least."

She hoped he was right. Lake Endwell was a small community. Claire biked everywhere, including the quaint downtown, the veterinary clinic, the church and her father's house. Most of Lake Endwell was within two miles of her home. She drove to volunteer at the zoo, though. The thirty-minute commute gave her time to think.

They neared her road, a narrow paved lane winding down to the lake. Large sections of newly cut tree trunks had been rolled to the shoulder. Dad's truck drove over smaller branches and leaves. Claire held her breath. Other than a flipped boat and some minor oddities, there didn't seem to be any severe damage. She leaned forward.

Granddad's huge old cabin rose proudly against the sparkling turquoise lake. Over sixty years old, the cabin with its hunter-green siding, white trim and white wrap-around decks still impressed. A spacious, welcoming vacation spot—she never tired of gazing at it from her porch next door. A driveway and lawn separated their properties. What she wouldn't give to wave to Granddad each morning, the way she had done when he was alive. Even when he became wheelchair bound, he lived in this beautiful home. The family made it completely handicap accessible so he could wake up to his view of the lake every morning. After he died, it became the go-to place for any out-of-town guests.

Claire's smaller, butter-yellow cottage came into view.

Still standing. She let out the breath she'd been holding. The window boxes Dad had built last year spilled pink and purple petunias, giving it the homey air she adored. He cut the engine, and, muscles protesting, she shot out of her seat. The sun warmed her face as she raced to the back fence, fumbled with the handle and charged into the backyard, stopping short.

What a mess.

The winds had wreaked havoc back here. The entire forest seemed to have fallen on her lawn, and her two lounge chairs had disappeared. The patio umbrella dangled upside down against the corner of the fence.

No signs of the otters. Her heart dropped to her stomach.

She would not panic.

They were here. They had to be here.

She ran to the cellar, hoping, praying. Down the slippery, damp concrete steps, into the cool darkness. She waited for her eyes to adjust. Her gut clenched. *Please...*

There. In the corner, Hansel and Gretel slept, all curled around each other. Quietly, she went to them, softly petting each to confirm they were alive. Hansel lifted his head, his nose high in the air, and yawned before tucking back under Gretel's body. Their distinctive musk brought tears to Claire's eyes.

"Well, hello to you too." She grinned, straightening. "I can see the storm didn't bother either of you."

A loud noise brought her back up the cellar steps. The small pond would need to be cleared of leaves and sticks, but she could safely leave the otters alone. Shading her eyes, she looked up—Dad had already found the ladder, climbed to her roof and was pounding loose shingles back in place.

"This will only take a minute, Claire. You don't want

these flapping off in the next storm. Why don't you go in and grab something to eat? Or better yet, go to bed."

Her stomach growled. How long had it been since she last ate?

At the welcome sight of her living room, her sanctuary, her knees almost buckled. She'd sit a minute. Just a minute.

Unable to fight her sheer lack of energy, she sank into the couch. A million worries raced. Although the wedding made Claire wary, she sympathized with Libby. It would be terrible to come so close only to have a tornado destroy the plans. Claire would bring her some flowers and brownies and let her cry on her shoulder for half the night if need be. She would be there for Libby, the way she always was and always would be.

And what about Reed? Stuck in the hospital, far away from home. At least he had his parents and Jake.

She burrowed deeper into the pillow. Reed was going to need a lot of care. The cast, wheelchair…pain.

A guy like him always got snatched up, but yesterday, Aunt Sally told her he was single. Claire yawned. Single, schmingle. Who cared? She'd thumped the final nail in her romantic-notions coffin long ago. If Justin hadn't convinced her to give up on men, Dr. Jerk Face had. *A Tuesday girl…*

Nope. Wasn't going there.

Images from last night danced in her mind—hanging the balloons, the comfortable feeling she always got in Uncle Joe's Restaurant, Reed coming in dripping wet, the sirens…

The rest swirled like the storm that held them hostage until she fell asleep.

If Reed had to guess, he'd say his ankle resembled one of the bloated balloons in Macy's Thanksgiving Day Parade. Snoopy, probably. The swelling pressed against the inside of his cast, a painful reminder of his captivity. His foot felt as though it weighed at least seven hundred pounds. When would it stop throbbing?

"Claire, do you still have those yoga blocks?" Sally, the barely five-foot-tall woman who could command an army general, stepped away from the couch with a throw pillow in hand. She fluffed it twice. Dale, Claire's dad, was doing who knew what in the bedroom. This was the weirdest Monday morning Reed had spent in…well…ever.

"Yoga blocks? What are those?" Dale's voice carried. "We need more hangers. I've got three shirts to hang up and no hangers."

Claire poked her head in through the open sliding door, where she swept twigs and leaves off the deck. "The blocks are in my closet. Should I get them?"

"Yes, and grab a bunch of hangers while you're at it." Sally wore jeans rolled up at the ankles and a Race for the Cure T-shirt. Flamingo earrings grazed her shoulders.

"Okay, I'll be right back." Claire disappeared.

"Yoga blocks, Dale," Sally's voice echoed as she tucked the pillow behind Reed's neck. "You remember—those blue foam dealies from last year when Libby convinced her to take Marissa's class."

Reed studied the cottage's living area. Streams of sunlight flooded the hardwood floors, and the warm lake breeze tickled the edges of the white sheer curtains. If he wasn't in so much pain, he'd like it here. Well, he'd like it better if the Sheffields weren't making such a fuss.

Sally hovered over him. The woman seemed to be everywhere at once. She and Dale were clearly siblings—Reed had never seen two people with so much energy.

"How are you feeling?" Sally brushed his hair from his forehead. "Do you want a drink? A painkiller?"

Reed inhaled with a hiss. He wanted to tell her he was fine. He didn't need yoga blocks—whatever they were. Or tender motherly touches. Or pillows behind his head. But the skyrocketing throbs prevented him from speaking. He shook his head, not even attempting to smile.

Sally made a clucking noise. "You don't need to suffer. I'm getting one of those pills."

Dale trekked back into the living room. "Marissa... Marissa... Oh, you mean the Schneider girl? She teaches yoga? Huh. They still taking the class?"

"Nope. Claire hated it." With a glass in one hand and a prescription bottle in the other, Sally pivoted around the kitchen counter. "Marissa got on some odd hot yoga bandwagon. Claire said it made her too sweaty. And Libby didn't want to do it without Claire." She handed Reed a pill and the water, then stood there until he had no choice but to swallow it. She stacked pillows under Reed's cast for the eighth time, propping his aching foot up. "Reed, you need to wiggle your toes."

He gripped the edge of the cushion. No way he was putting his foot in more agony.

"Come on, now. Wiggle those toes. Don't make me call the doctor."

"Fine." Reed concentrated until the big toe moved. A flash of heat spread through his torso, and a bead of sweat dripped down his temple past his ear.

"Good job!" Sally said. "Keep moving them whenever you think of it. You'll heal faster."

Dale hustled to the kitchen—the living room, kitchen and dining room were one large open space—and rummaged through a drawer. "His suitcase is unpacked. Should I stop at the store? Get some groceries?" Paper in hand, he returned to stand next to Sally and clicked a pen. "Tell me what he needs."

"Crackers, soda, things that are easy on the stomach. Doubt he'll want much to eat today. I'm sure he'll have more of an appetite tomorrow."

Reed ground his teeth together. Why were they talking about him as if he weren't there?

"Reed?" Sally leaned over him. "We're going to the store. What can we get you?"

His head swam. "My phone and laptop."

She laughed. "You don't need those. You need to rest. I meant, what kind of food do you like—snacks, soda, fruit? We'll get it for you."

"You don't have to—"

"Oh, hush. There's no stopping us. Help us make up this list, and we'll get out of your hair for a while so you can sleep."

Dale cleared his throat. "I'll get your phone and your laptop."

"He shouldn't be working." Sally narrowed her eyes at Dale.

"The man needs his electronics." Dale disappeared again.

Reed's neck relaxed. Dale had just gone up a notch in his book.

"Let's start with produce. Bananas? Apples? Watermelon?" Sally hashed out a grocery list at least fifty items too long, but she kept naming off foods and wouldn't listen to Reed's objections.

Dale dragged the coffee table closer to the couch, plugged in Reed's laptop and set his phone on the table. "Need any help before we take off?"

Reed shook his head.

"Take a nap," Sally said. "And keep wiggling those toes."

She walked to the front door with Dale at her heels. They kept up a steady stream of conversation all the way out. Reed moved his toes once more. Broke out in another sweat at the effort. Then he stared at the vaulted wooden ceiling.

Trapped.

In more ways than one.

The car ride from the hospital to the cottage had been agonizing. Every bump, every turn, every tap on the breaks ignited his leg. The jolting wheelchair ride up the ramp to the cabin had sent him to level nine on the pain scale. And moving him to the couch? He might be stuck in this exact position for two weeks, because he was not going through that torture again.

"Yoo-hoo." Claire sailed in through the front door. "I've got the blocks."

"You just missed them." Reed twisted his neck to watch her. She wore a white T-shirt with I Love My Zoo in black letters. He pointed at her face. "The bruise under your eye is turning purple."

"Yeah, I try to coordinate my injuries with my clothes. Less need for makeup." She swiped her hand down the air in front of her lavender running shorts. "You like?"

He did like. And he'd smile but his leg tortured him. The painkillers could not kick in soon enough.

"I'm not sure what Aunt Sally wants with these." Claire held a large paper bag with blue foam peeking out and a bundle of hangers. "But I've learned not to ask questions. The woman is a master. Hey, does your dad know you were released this morning? I didn't even think to call him. Should I call him now?"

"No!" The word came out sharper than he intended. "I mean, no, it's Monday, right? He's at work. I'll call him later."

"Yes, it's Monday." A quizzical look flashed across her face, but she brightened. "Okay. So I'm sure Jake's told you the latest wedding drama."

Jake hadn't, but Reed wasn't ready to admit it. He'd play along. "What's Libby take on it?"

Claire plopped into the tan chair kitty-corner from the

couch. "Let's say the idea of a cake-only reception didn't go well."

"Why only cake?" He had no experience with weddings or much of anything besides his job and the parks in the Chicago vicinity. His mountain bike had seen them all. How long would it be until he could ride again?

"Uncle Joe's Restaurant is closed indefinitely. Every other hall is booked. The church is too. So their options have dwindled." She rubbed her arm, concern in her eyes.

"What are they going to do?"

"I'm not sure. Libby and I spent so much time getting all the details perfect—it will be hard for her to let go."

Reed's cell phone rang. His boss. "Claire, do you mind if I take this?"

"Of course not! I'll finish sweeping the deck and give you some privacy. I've got to take off for work in a little bit anyway."

Before he answered, Reed admired her as she disappeared outside. The phone rang again.

Boss. Phone. Right.

"Reed here."

"Hey, how far have you made it?" John's hearty voice was the healthy dose of normal Reed needed. Fifteen years older than Reed, John Dalton was more a mentor and friend than boss. "You must be in Minnesota by now, or wait, North Dakota."

"Change in plans." Reed winced as he shifted to sit up. "Get this. A tornado roared through town Friday night. No wedding. And no Alaska."

"What? Why?"

"Broken leg. I'm hanging out in Lake Endwell a week or so. Just until I'm out of the wheelchair."

"Wheelchair?" John sucked in a throaty breath. "I can't believe it. Everyone else okay?"

"Yeah, I heard the town got hit pretty hard, though, so

I'm going to do what I can to help organize crews until I get back. You have any leads for this area?"

"I'll look into it." Papers shuffled in the background. "How are things with your dad?"

"As awkward as usual."

"Sorry. For what it's worth, I give you credit. Maybe you'll work it out while you're there."

"I doubt it." Reed flexed his fingers. "You might as well have Cranston send me the monthly reports. Oh, and the forms he told me about. It'll give me a chance to get familiar with the new position. If I'm stuck on the couch, I want to be doing something."

John chuckled. "Always working, aren't you? I'll send them, but focus on getting that leg healed. And I'll call you when I get more info about contractors down there."

They said goodbye and hung up. Reed tapped the phone against his chin. Two raps on the glass door had him hitching his chin for Claire to enter.

"Well, my work is done here." She grinned and dusted off the front of her shorts. "Anything I can get you before I head to work?"

"Should you be working today? You're still pretty beat up."

Her cheeks sagged. "My boss expects me there. But I'll come back over tonight." She drifted to him, and he found himself holding his breath. What was she doing? She grabbed his cell phone, swiped it and a minute later, set it on the coffee table. "There. I programmed my number. You need anything, text me, okay?"

"Wait." He didn't want her to go. Not yet. "Have you seen the restaurant?"

"No." She frowned and sat in the chair. "The dining room survived, but not much else. At least that's what I'm hearing. I'm not sure I want to see for myself."

"I'm glad part of it is still standing."

"I am too." Uncertainty shone in her eyes. "What if it needs to be torn down? I don't like to think of it in shambles, but I'll take shambles over nonexistent."

"A good builder wouldn't tear it down unless it was absolutely necessary."

"That's what I'm worried about." She twisted her hands together and bit her lower lip. "If I asked for a favor…"

A favor? What kind of favor? His stomach tightened, but her pleading eyes broke through his defenses. He wanted to help.

"I know you're hurt and won't be here long, but could you help Aunt Sally and Uncle Joe find a good contractor?"

He exhaled in relief. "If they need help, of course. I've worked with disaster relief crews in the past, and red tape can hold up projects for months."

"What do you mean by red tape?"

"Getting the insurance adjusters, builders and business owners to agree on costs and schedules is no easy task." Pain spread from his ankle again. "Let's hope there won't be any problems, and the work will get started right away."

Claire stood, rubbing her arm. "But what if there are problems?"

"I know how to get things moving."

Smiling, she grazed his hand with her fingertips. "Thank you. And I insist on helping in any way I can." She checked her watch. "Oh! I've got to go. Get some rest, okay?"

She glided through the kitchen and let herself out.

He lay back against the pillows. The thought of working with Claire set off warning alarms, but he dismissed them. He'd be back home in a week. All he had to do was focus on rebuilding the town, and no one would get hurt.

Chapter Three

❧

"Really, Claire? I shouldn't have to tell you this."

Claire took a deep breath before turning to Tammy Lathrop—Dr. Tammy—the boss she never seemed to please. The small examination room at the clinic smelled of wet dog, cleaner and dog biscuits, which usually didn't bother Claire, but today the medley of scents closed in on her. The fact that she should have been home thirty minutes ago didn't help. Eight hours on her feet every Monday was bad enough—today's tally would be closer to nine.

Tammy gestured to the bottle of cleaner in Claire's hand. "You know we use the sanitizer solution with bleach to clean the examination tables."

"This is the sanitizer solution with bleach." Claire tried to remain pleasant.

"No, it isn't. That's the blue bottle. You need to get the purple bottle."

"They repackaged it." She held it up. "The bleach solution looks like this now."

Tammy stared, her jaw tightening. "Let me see it." She waved two fingers for Claire to hand it to her. After reading the label, Tammy thrust it back in Claire's hand. "Fine. But wipe it down twice. It looks like you missed a spot over there."

Claire strangled the paper towel in her hand until her boss exited. She couldn't do this much longer. She never minded cleaning up after patients, but when her every move was judged and criticized, it killed her morale.

Tammy hadn't even asked about her black eye or scratches. There had been a time Tammy would be the first to show concern. She probably would have urged Claire to take the day off. But those days had disappeared long ago when Tammy started seeing Mark Calloway, aka Dr. Jerk Face.

So Claire had worked for Mark before Tammy. Was it really that big a deal that Claire dated him briefly? Apparently. But Claire had dumped him, not the other way around, and Mark had promptly spread rumors about her around town. No doubt, Mark filled Tammy's head with the same lies. An ex ruining another good thing in her life—a friendship she'd cherished. A job she liked. It still hurt.

Not that Tammy was worth it if she believed everything he said.

Claire sprayed and wiped the examination table. Getting Reed settled next door this morning had taken her mind off the job opening at the zoo. Last night, after she, Dad and her brothers cleaned up the yard for the otters, Claire had finished her online application. The only red flag? The omission of recent job references. Mark certainly wouldn't give her one. And Claire didn't want Tammy to know she was actively job hunting. Hopefully, her volunteer work at the zoo and the letter from her friend, Lisa Jones, who owned the animal sanctuary where Claire gave free check-ups to injured birds and animals, would be enough.

Submitting the application had been exhilarating, but now the giddiness melted into anxiety. Were her qualifications enough? Had she answered the questions correctly?

One of the zookeepers had texted her at lunch. Did you put your app in yet? I heard Tina say she has 30 in already.

Claire continued wiping the surfaces. Thirty applications. And the job had been posted on Friday. Steep competition.

Working quickly and methodically, she finished cleaning the room. She put the supplies away and found her purse, and she and the receptionist left together. A blast of moist heat hit her as she made her way to her bike. A breeze to keep her scrubs from clinging to her skin couldn't be too much to ask for, could it?

She pedaled down the side street to a back road—her favorite route home. Varying shades of green leaves dotted the woods on either side, and a pair of mourning doves swooped ahead of her. Her legs tightened, burned, but she forced them to keep pumping up the hill. The exertion burned off some of her earlier resentment.

After she'd changed into shorts and fed the otters, Claire stood outside Granddad's cottage. Aunt Sally had texted her earlier to say she had plans tonight but that she'd left stir-fry ingredients in Reed's fridge.

Preparing dinner for Reed didn't sound like a good time. For one, she was a lousy cook. Two, making food seemed intimate, and after this morning when her treacherous body betrayed her—she'd practically gotten shivers putting her phone number in Reed's cell—she'd promised herself to be nurselike. Detached.

One-on-one interactions with a devastatingly gorgeous guy? One on his way back to Chicago soon? Not smart.

She knocked and strolled inside. From across the room, she noted Reed's paleness. Reclining on the sofa, eyes closed with his cast up on her yoga blocks—Aunt Sally had hit a home run again—Reed's slack face looked haggard while he slept. Poor guy.

As quietly as possible, she padded to him and pressed

the back of her hand against his forehead. No fever. But his shallow breathing indicated his discomfort even in sleep.

She retreated to the kitchen and cut up the vegetables. Started the rice. Heated oil in the pan and added chicken breast chunks. When they began to sizzle, she seasoned and stirred them. A moan from the couch spun her attention to the living room.

"Hey, how are you feeling?" Claire set the spatula on the counter and went to Reed. "What can I get you? Do you need help with anything?"

He blew out a breath and ran his hand through his hair, leaving it more rumpled than before. More tempting. "The chair. Help me into the wheelchair."

She kneeled, setting his arm around her shoulder as he swung his legs to the side. He hissed.

"I'm sorry." She touched his hard, muscular biceps. Big mistake. Warmth pooled in her stomach. "Did I hurt you?"

"No," he said through clenched teeth.

It took a few minutes and more exertion than she anticipated, but they succeeded in getting him into the chair. He slowly wheeled down the hall.

"Do you need me to help you?" she called after him.

"No. Got it."

An acrid smell came from the kitchen. She jogged to the stove. The chicken had taken on a dark brown hue, but the chunks weren't officially burned…just well done. Very well done. Stirring the rice, she realized she'd forgotten to cover the pan or put it on low, so a crispy layer coated the bottom.

She broke up the chunks, added a bit more water and hoped it would be edible.

Several minutes later she spooned rice and the chicken-and-vegetable mixture onto a plate, then shimmied past the counter to see what was keeping Reed.

"Are you okay?" She stretched her neck to see down the hall. Empty.

"Fine."

"Need me to help?"

"No." His voice sounded strained.

Should she stay? Help him? Or set the food on the table and leave?

"Your dinner is on the table," she called.

"Okay."

"Want me to stay?"

A clamor came from the hall. Reed wheeled back to her, the paleness in his face replaced by brick red. "You don't have to. I'll be fine."

She hesitated. He didn't look fine. But she didn't want to intrude. And as much as her nursing instincts prodded her to monitor him, her feminine instincts hollered to get back home. Stat.

"I'll eat with you and get you settled." She pulled another plate out of the cupboard. Reed moved to the end of the table where she'd set his food.

Joining him, she bowed her head, said grace and motioned to his fork. "Go ahead." She bit down on a too-crunchy piece of broccoli. The flavors in her mouth created an odd mixture of char, salt and teriyaki sauce. She almost spit it out. "This is disgusting. I'm making you a sandwich."

He'd paled again. But he hadn't touched his food, so dinner wasn't to blame.

"Maybe you should lie down." She bit her lower lip.

Nodding, he pushed himself back to the couch. She helped him get settled. He winced as she set his cast back onto the yoga blocks. "I'll let you rest."

"No, wait." His hand darted out and clasped her wrist, sending awareness up her spine. "Stay."

How could she refuse an injured man? One with eyes

the exact brown of Gretel's fur? Who'd put his life at risk to protect her? She gulped. One who…needed her?

Her downfall.

There went her good intentions to be nurselike. Detached.

Because being needed was her weakest spot. Always had been. Always would be.

Reed groaned. Why had he asked Claire to stay? When he was supposed to be focused on anything but her?

He was a needy mess, that was why.

"Of course I'll stay." Claire adjusted the pillow behind his neck, then sat in the leather chair. "Tomorrow, I'll take you out on the deck. The fresh air will do you good."

Fresh air or a slap in the face. Anything to get him rational again.

He searched for a safe topic to discuss. "What's it like living here?" There. He'd be reminded of why Lake Endwell was the last place on earth he belonged. No skyscrapers, Wrigley Field, world-class museums—not that he ever went to any—gourmet restaurants or the Chicago Bears.

Claire smiled at him. "Good question. I'm not sure how to answer. It's home. Dinners with my family right here in this cottage. Aunt Sally and Uncle Joe always cook. It's barbecues, boat rides, bicycling around town. Ice cream at Tastee Freeze. Fourth of July picnic. A big Christmas tree–lighting ceremony in City Park by the gazebo."

"Sounds idyllic."

Her eyes twinkled. "When we were little, Dad took us kids to Cookie's Diner on Saturday mornings. I always got hot chocolate and toast. I'd spread grape jelly on one slice and strawberry on the other. Cookie's went out of business, so we all go to Pat's Diner now. It's one of the few buildings unaffected by the tornado. Thankfully, the church didn't get touched either."

"Do you still get hot chocolate and toast?"

She laughed. Reminded him of little bells. Happiness. "No. Omelets or pancakes for me. With a side of bacon. And coffee. Lots of coffee."

"My kind of breakfast." His leg hardly bothered him now. If she would just keep talking… "Tell me about the town. How bad does Main Street look?"

She shook her head, lifting her eyes to the ceiling. "Terrible. I don't know how to process it. My favorite places are surrounded by piles of bricks and smashed windows. I mean, I got my ears pierced at JoJo's Jewelry. Mom and Aunt Sally took me, and boy, was I excited! Mom held my hand the whole time. She died giving birth to Libby. It's hard to have another link to her disappear, you know?"

Yeah. He did know. "My mom died when I was seven." His links to her were long gone, and his memories weren't that great to begin with. "How old were you?"

"I was six. You lost your mom too? Mine died of a postpartum hemorrhage. I still miss her. What happened to yours?"

"Car accident." He'd learned to keep the story simple. It had been bad enough getting badgered by his classmates at school. Everyone whispered about it. The paper had spared no gory detail. Except no one knew the real reason why. Just him and Dad. Kind of.

She leaned over and squeezed his hand. He felt her touch all the way to his heart.

"I was blessed to have a little brother and baby sister to take care of. After the funeral, I promised to be the mom Libby and Sam needed. I tried to help my older brothers too, but the little ones needed me more. Aunt Sally really stepped in for us. She made sure we had the advice Mom would have given. I don't know what I would have done without her."

"You were a little kid. No one expected you to be their mother."

She shrugged. "I know. But I had six wonderful years with Mom. Those two didn't know her. I wanted to be there for them—for her sake. Did you have family step in and help out after your mom passed?"

He shifted his jaw. Usually, this was the point in the conversation he cracked a joke and changed the subject, but maybe it would be better for Claire to know the truth. Part of it anyway.

"No, they didn't." He folded his hands, let them rest on his abdomen. "In fact, after the funeral, Mom's family acted like I didn't exist. No more birthday parties or family get-togethers. My grandmother, who I spent a lot of time with as a kid, pretended she didn't know me one day when we ran into her at the grocery store. We moved to another town a few months later."

Claire's mouth dropped open. "What? How could she? You were a little boy. I want to go there and give her a piece of my mind."

He hadn't expected her righteous indignation. "You can't. I heard she died a few years ago. I got over it."

"Well, I'm not getting over it. Families are supposed to stick together and support each other."

"That's why I don't do families. I like being my own person. And I've worked hard to move up in Rockbend Construction. Chicago is big and fun, and I belong there. It's home for me the way Lake Endwell is for you."

Claire crossed one leg over the other. "So you're not into family? What about your dad and Jake?"

"Jake's great. Best kid in the world."

"And your dad?"

He hesitated. How much should he reveal to her? "We're fine. Not close, but we're fine."

"Well, someday you'll want a family of your own." She stared out the windows at the lake.

"Nah, I'm good." He'd lost people who had meant the world to him. Mom would never come back. Her family refused to acknowledge he existed. Dad barely talked to him after her death. And then there was Collin.

She gave him a sharp look. "Really?"

"Really."

Her shoulder lifted. "I feel the same. I've got all I need."

"You? Not having a family of your own?" He guffawed. "I find that hard to believe."

Sadness draped her eyes, but she hid it quickly. "Believe it."

"Why?"

"One, I'm not moving again, and the pickings around here are slim. And two, I have high expectations. I haven't met a man willing to put me first. Anyway, I'm happy with my life the way it is."

Her first reason put the brakes on his speeding attraction. The second? Made him squirm. She deserved to be first in a man's life.

Too bad he wasn't capable of being that man.

Chapter Four

Claire tossed her keys on the kitchen counter, tried to work the kinks out of her neck and strode to the patio door. Another boring Wednesday at work, and now she had to come up with something edible to bring to Reed's. Why had Aunt Sally chosen tonight to get her hair trimmed and colored?

"Hey, babies, where are you?" Claire called. The otters raced to her, their long bodies undulating across the lawn. She gave them each a carrot and stroked their thick, soft fur. Their mild scent teased her nose. Gretel got up on her hind legs and sniffed, then made a funny snorting sound. "No, you get one carrot tonight, little lady. You know the drill."

They loved fresh vegetables and fruits, but their main diet consisted of fish supplied by the zoo, with an occasional crawfish, frog or boiled egg. Gretel nudged Claire's hand with her nose. She laughed, shaking her head. "I'll bring you apples tomorrow. You're incorrigible."

Claire lay back in the lounge chair and mindlessly observed the clouds drifting across the sky. Spending time with Hansel and Gretel made up a little for what she'd had to deal with at the clinic today. Once again, passed over to assist Tammy in an operation. Put on cat-cage cleaning duty. This made three weeks in a row.

She blew out a breath. She deserved better. If she didn't get the position at the zoo, she would have to make some changes. Life was too short to work for someone who treated her like garbage.

The otters stretched out in the sun for a nap. She'd wasted enough time thinking about her thankless job. A more important topic loomed.

Reed. She'd checked on him the past two evenings, but Aunt Sally had been keeping vigil, and Reed had been asleep both times. Her dad helped Reed with basic care off and on during the day.

Claire couldn't get Reed out of her mind. And she needed to. He'd made it clear his home was in Chicago.

What he'd revealed about his mom's death—how his family treated him—still filled her with indignation. How could anyone disown a child? How painful it must have been for him to lose his mom and her family.

Her chest burned the more she thought about it. No wonder he wasn't into families. She probably wouldn't be either if she'd gone through what he had. And it made her wonder about Reed's dad. Roger hadn't come over to check on Reed. Aunt Sally said Jake stopped by last night. But not his own father? Strange.

Claire plodded inside to change. Her cooking skills clearly qualified her for the title of Worst Cook in America. At this point, a grilled cheese might be too much to hope for.

The phone rang as she shimmied into her khaki shorts.

"How's my favorite niece?" Uncle Joe asked, not waiting for her to answer. "Sally got home early and made you and Reed dinner if you want to swing by and pick it up."

Claire almost purred. "You two are lifesavers. How did you know I dreaded having to deal with dinner?"

"You never want to deal with dinner." His raspy chuckle made her smile. "And you know your aunt. She lives to feed people. With the restaurant shut down, she's going crazy. If she's not cooking, she's pestering."

"Well, tell her not to stop," she said. "I'll be right there. Don't let any of my cousins steal my food either. I know how they are."

Claire slipped into her favorite sparkly black flip-flops, grabbed her purse and drove the mile to Uncle Joe and Aunt Sally's house. Nestled on a wooded property, the ranch-style home hid behind a grove of evergreens. Claire parked next to her cousin's beat-up truck and then loped to the front door. With a quick knock, she let herself in, calling, "It's me."

"Come on in." Aunt Sally beamed from behind the kitchen counter. The smell of fried chicken made Claire's stomach rumble. Aunt Sally pushed a plate of cheese and crackers toward her. "Don't worry, I didn't let Braedon touch your takeout containers."

They had a running joke that Braedon, her twenty-five-year-old cousin who regularly stopped by for dinner, could eat a sumo wrestler under the table. Claire nibbled on a cracker. "Your hair looks fabulous. Have you heard anything about the restaurant? When do you think it will re-open?"

"Thanks, hon." She fluffed her bangs. "The insurance adjuster hasn't been out, but he told us to use their contractor. We've called the guy and keep getting a machine. I don't like that we can't pick our own builder. We need the restaurant up and running. Where will everyone go for Friday fish fry? And now that the weather's gotten nice, people are looking to eat on the patio by the lake. I don't know what we'll do if we can't get opened again soon."

Claire hated to think of the restaurant shut down indefinitely, but she hadn't gotten the nerve up to go back and see the damage for herself. The other night a sound from the television reminded her of the roof tearing off, and it had taken her ten minutes to calm down. "I'm praying."

"Thanks." Sally sniffed. "We don't have it as bad as most of the folks around here. Lois and Herb moved to a hotel twenty minutes away until their house gets fixed, and I don't know how those Riley sisters are doing it, living with half a roof. Don't get me started on Miss Gert."

"Miss Gert? Is Whiskers still missing?" Claire selected another cheese cube. "I thought Dad formed a search party." Miss Gert was eighty-four, lived in a house so old it could have been built by Christopher Columbus himself and doted on her long-haired, extremely pudgy cat.

"Oh, they found him all right. Eating a dead bird in that ramshackle barn behind her place. But she can't keep Whiskers inside with her back room damaged. She'll have a heart attack worrying. I told Dale to get some of the boys together and patch it up for her, but she thinks the noise will hurt poor Whiskers's ears."

"Want me to go over and talk to her? Maybe I can take her to the grocery store or something while they do a quick repair job."

"Would you?" Aunt Sally beamed. "I'd do it myself, but you know she can't stand me. She aimed that BB gun of hers at my head last time I tried to bring her lunch."

Claire laughed. "I'll do my best. And let's hope the insurance people and builders get things done quickly."

"Reed's boss called him while I was there yesterday. No calls have come through from any girls. I'd say he's definitely girlfriend free." Sally gave her a knowing look, then handed her the takeout bag. "You'd better get moving if you want to enjoy your meal while it's hot. Tell Reed hi for us, and let him know I'll be bringing lunch tomorrow around noon. I like that boy. He's respectful and cute."

Claire couldn't deny it. He *was* cute.

"Nothing to say, huh?" Sally popped a hand on her hip. "Hey, I may be getting older, but I'm not blind. I'll gladly bring a handsome guy lunch every day. Yes, I will. And I think you should make the most of this opportunity. A fine man like him hasn't come through town in years."

Claire wasn't touching this conversation with a fly-fishing rod.

"How's he been with you? Not much of a talker, is he?"

"He talks," Claire said. "He's probably in pain and doesn't want to show it."

"I'm sure you're right. With you bringing him dinner, maybe we can convince him to stay."

Not likely. "I think he's pretty happy in Chicago." Claire reached for the handles of the paper bag. She kissed her aunt on the cheek, thanked her and headed back to Granddad's cottage.

Five minutes later, as she made her way up the ramp, she paused to savor the low sunlight spreading gold over the lake. Her favorite place in the world. God had touched this land, blessed it with beauty. Giving the side door a perfunctory two knocks, she cracked it open.

"Yoo-hoo, Reed? It's Claire." She set the bag on the large island and continued to the living room, stopping when she glimpsed him.

Shirtless.

Her mouth dried to ashes. Wow. Reed's arms flailed over his head, and the T-shirt he wrestled with tangled in his hands and forearms. He muttered something, and she chortled, choking on a laugh as she sped to his side.

"Let me." She tugged the cotton off him, and then, trying not to gawk at his bare chest—she'd be attempting to erase the image of that six-pack for some time, maybe forever—she straightened the material and stretched it over his neck. She spun on her heel to return to the kitchen. Why was she out of breath?

"When you're ready, come to the table." Her words came out higher-pitched than a three-year-old's.

Reed followed her. His face had reddened—embarrassment or exertion?—but he stopped the wheelchair at the low farmhouse table next to a bank of floor-to-ceiling windows.

"Isn't the view incredible? Another gorgeous day on the lake." She snatched two plates out of the cupboard, piled silverware and napkins on top and quickly set the table. Then she divvied up the fried chicken, mashed potatoes and gravy, corn and biscuits before taking a seat next to him. "Want me to say grace?"

"I'll do it." Reed folded his hands and said a prayer. When he finished, Claire smiled at him, but the hollowness in his eyes stopped her from digging into the food. "What's wrong?"

He sent a sharp glance her way. "Nothing."

"I didn't cook this." She backed her palms to her shoulders. "Aunt Sally did."

That brought the hint of a smile to his unshaven face.

"Is it your leg? The first week is the worst for pain. Have you been taking your meds?" She strolled to the counter and found the orange bottles of various medications he was supposed to be taking.

"I'm fine," he growled.

"You are not fine." She held up one of the bottles. "I can see it in your eyes. I'm a trained professional, you know."

"I'm not an animal."

She chuckled. "I know. My otters are more playful. You're grumpier."

"Your...what?" His crinkled nose and eyebrows reminded her she'd never told him about the rescued babies.

"Otters. I'm caring for twins until the zoo takes them later this summer."

"Why?"

"Their mom was attacked. Lost the use of her back legs. My friend Lisa runs an animal sanctuary nearby and was able to deliver the twins. They stayed with their mother until they were weaned, but Lisa only keeps injured animals. They're too tame to be released into the wild, so I made an arrangement with the zoo. I'm housing them until the new exhibit is ready next month." Finding the prescription ibuprofen, she returned to the table and slid the tablet his way. "Here. You should be a quarter way through the bottle by now. Haven't you taken any?"

"I don't need them." He pushed it away. "Before you start lecturing, though, I *have* been taking the antibiotics."

"I'm not lecturing." Technically, she *was* lecturing, but she preferred to think of it as reminding. "Now is not the time to play tough guy, Reed. The painkillers will make this easier on you."

The vein in his temple jumped. He ignored the pill and bit into his drumstick.

What now? She couldn't force him to take it. And she couldn't hide it in a piece of cheese the way she did when a pet stubbornly refused a tablet.

Well, she probably could hide it in a piece of cheese, but Reed was an adult. He could make his own decisions and live with the aftermath.

She suppressed a sigh and dug into her potatoes, telling him about Wompers, the enormous dog no one in their clinic had been able to budge from the waiting room this morning. The owner tried to drag the poor beast, but the dog could not be moved.

The dark circles under Reed's eyes and the tightness around his mouth churned her stomach.

"Just take the stinking pill." She pointed to it with her fork.

He glared for five seconds but finally popped it in his

mouth and took a swig of lemonade. She smiled. "That wasn't so hard, was it?"

They finished the meal in silence. When Claire stood to clear their plates, Reed backed the chair up, but it got caught on something. He jammed the wheels forward, then backward, then forward again. His body crackled with tension. "I hate this."

Claire wanted to go to him, put her arm around his shoulder and comfort him. But it wasn't her place.

"This stupid chair," he said. "I can barely get around."

"I would hate it too. I wish I could make your leg heal with the snap of my fingers." Claire strode to the living room and opened a cabinet. "Maybe you need something to take your mind off things."

She selected an early CD by Michael Bublé and slid it into the stereo. Jaunty music filled the air. Returning to the kitchen, she stacked dishes in the sink. Then she paused in the living room—Reed had wheeled to the sliding door and looked out at the lake. He rested his chin on his fist, his gaze faraway.

"As hard as it is for me right now, the view almost makes me forget. Your grandfather knew what he was doing when he made his home here."

"I'm glad you think so." The whitewashed walls, tan leather furniture, bookcases filled with paperbacks, old ashtrays and golden retriever knickknacks relaxed her. Reminded her how Granddad always had a hug and a pot of coffee for her. "It's been a big part of my life."

Reed's eyes appeared almost copper in the weakening light, and the expression in them... Apologetic? Or appreciative?

"Claire?" His long lashes lowered. "Will you help me out of this torture chamber so I can sit on the couch?"

"Of course." A slow ballad came on. She bent for him to put his arm around her shoulder and lifted as he heaved his body upward. The smell of his skin hinted at an ocean breeze. "There. Move to the left. Careful."

He reclined on the couch, his cheeks ruddy from exertion.

"Better?" She adjusted the yoga blocks under his cast.

"Yeah." He sounded hoarse. "Come here a minute."

She moved to his side, her pulse racing. Why did her skin feel prickly all of a sudden?

He took her hand, his thumb rubbing over her hers. "Can you stay awhile?"

"Yes." Her voice sounded like a tiny mouse's, if tiny mice could speak.

"Good."

For a split second, she thought he might want to kiss her. She wanted him to kiss her.

"Tell me what's going on with the town cleanup." He let her hand drop.

She blinked. See? He didn't want to kiss her. Just helping the town. Nothing more.

Claire crossed to the chair, a safe distance from him but close enough they could chat with ease. "Not much. The insurance adjuster hasn't been out to Uncle Joe's yet. On Sunday, a bunch of people cleared the street downtown to be drivable, but other than tarps covering a few houses, nothing is happening."

"We need to change that." His tone went from smooth to brisk. She liked smooth better. "Do you have a paper and pen? If we're going to get this town restored, I have questions to be answered."

"Really?" She scurried to the kitchen for pen and paper. When she returned, she clicked the pen, preparing to write. "What do you want to know?"

"What stores would you say need the most work?"

She thought a moment and listed the ones she could think of. "Let me call Dad. He knows more than I do."

Pulling her cell phone from her pocket, she dialed his number. "Dad? Reed and I are making a list of all the stores destroyed—"

"Good idea. I'll be right there." He hung up before she could respond.

She shrugged, smiling at Reed. "Dad's on his way."

The corner of his mouth twisted. "You mean I don't get you all to myself?"

All to himself? Claire widened her eyes and shrugged.

Then he grinned. "Your dad's great. I want to make as many calls as possible before I leave next week."

And just like that, her spirits dropped to the floor. Next week would be here before she knew it, and playing with temptation had burned her twice before. Not this time.

Five more minutes. Five minutes and he was sawing the cast off. He'd use a butter knife if he had to.

Reed gripped the arms of the wheelchair. The itch in his leg permeated his thoughts. A thin branch taunted from the limb overhanging the deck. If Reed went outside and snapped the twig, he'd jam it in his cast and scrape his leg until no skin remained.

Fridays were supposed to be good days. Fun days. But after two hours of studying the weekly report he would be in charge of as vice president, he'd almost fallen asleep of boredom. So he'd switched gears, making phone calls to local business owners, construction crews and even two insurance adjusters. Right up his alley. But, with nothing more to do, Reed had thumbed through every magazine in the cottage. Knew all the summer fashions. Skimmed the bookcases and learned about the war of 1812. Memorized the capitals of the fifty states. The television bored him. Inactivity? A cruel, cruel fate.

Knock, knock. The side door opened.

"Guess what we're having for lunch? Lobster pasta salad

and my famous BLTs with avocado sauce." Sally breezed into the kitchen. Knocks were clearly cursory in Lake Endwell. At least this time Reed was fully dressed. "Give me a minute and I'll have everything ready."

He never guessed how difficult it would be to do the most simple of tasks on his own. Dale stopped by each morning, helping Reed wrap his cast in a plastic bag and tape it so he could take a shower. Dale also showed him how to maneuver the wheelchair to get down to the dock—an exhausting undertaking Reed wouldn't be attempting on his own anytime soon.

Yesterday had brought Reed to an all-time low. He'd slammed his fingers in the drawer trying to get out a spoon, and when his cell phone fell to the floor midcall with John, it had taken him ten minutes to pick it back up. Barbara had called late in the afternoon to check on him, and he still winced at how terse he'd been. But, come on, why couldn't Dad call? Why did it always have to be her?

And what about the other night when Claire had trotted into the living room and caught him wrestling with a T-shirt? He'd wanted nothing more than to wheel himself into the lake and be done with it. Naturally, he'd poured the charm on by acting like a baby and refusing pain meds.

No wonder he lived alone.

Sally fussed with the food on the counter. "...and you and I are going to eat outside. It's too nice out to be cooped up all the time. I brought some cards. I only know Go Fish, so if you're looking for something fancy, I'm not your gal. Oh, and I brought some gossip mags. Look." She brandished a magazine with celebrities on the cover. "It's got all the pictures of the stars without makeup. I think she looks like an absolute hag."

She tossed the magazine on his lap. He held it up. The picture must have been altered. The actress *did* look like a hag.

"Come on, don't be shy." Balancing two plastic plates in her hands, she used her hip to slide the glass patio door open. "It's warm out here. I'll launch the umbrella."

He had little choice but to follow, and, frankly, he'd promised himself he would make more of an effort with everyone. Except Claire. Every time she came over, he wanted her to stay longer. And he couldn't stop staring at her. Drawn to her easygoing personality. Blinded by her baby blues.

She'd made it clear as the lake in front of him that she needed a man to put her first. Here. In Lake Endwell.

He was not that man.

But…he anticipated the way her face lit up when she waltzed in the door. Enjoyed the lilt of the "Yoo-hoo" she called to announce herself. Could listen to her tales of dogs and cats and otters all day long. Kind of had a hard time looking away from her sparkly tank tops with various sayings on them like yesterday's Zoo Freak.

Whenever he glimpsed her lips, he wanted to kiss her.

Sally set the plates on the patio table. "I'm experimenting with different flavors of iced tea. Do you like kiwi?" She cranked the umbrella until it soared over them.

"Uh, yes." Good. A distraction. "I do like kiwi."

"Great. I'll be right back. You go ahead and start in on the sandwich. You're probably starving."

He wasn't hungry, but the food did make his mouth water. Sally was an amazing cook.

"Here you are." She took the seat opposite him then grunted. "Why haven't you eaten?"

"I thought I'd wait for you."

"Aw, that's why I like you." For a minute he thought she might pinch his cheek, but she didn't. "Since you're looking livelier today, why don't you tell me about yourself. What's it like to live in Chicago?"

In between bites of the most delicious bacon, lettuce

and tomato sandwich he'd ever tasted, he filled her in on his job and the work he'd put in to become vice president. When she asked about life outside of work, he told her how much he enjoyed mountain biking and watching his beloved Chicago Bears, and he filled her in on his canceled Alaska trip.

"So, Sally." He pushed his empty plate away. "What's the word on the restaurant?"

Sally tossed her napkin on the table in disgust. "The word is nothing. We're not getting anywhere with this contractor. I've called at least fifteen times. All I get is a recording."

Reed frowned. Almost a week and they hadn't even talked to the builder? "Give me the name of the company and your rep. I'll see if your insurance will pay for a different contractor."

"Oh, honey, I don't want you lifting a finger right now. You worry about your leg. We'll worry about the restaurant."

He laughed. "It's not lifting a finger. It's swiping one. Give me the number. I want to help."

"Well, bless your heart. I'm taking you up on it."

A flash of red caught his eye. "Isn't that Claire's bike? What's she doing home?"

Sally crossed to the side rail. "Sure is. I'll go see." Before Sally made it to the patio door, Claire had raced up the deck ramp. Her chest heaved and her eyes flashed. Her Garfield scrubs shouldn't have made his throat go dry, but she could have worn a garbage bag and been the prettiest girl he'd ever seen.

"What on earth is wrong?" Sally asked.

"I got canned." Claire practically throbbed with pent-up energy. Her dark hair fell past her shoulders in windswept fury. She marched to the table and sprawled in a chair. "Yeah, apparently I missed a nugget in a kitty-litter box—a gross oversight on my part, which didn't even happen! I've never, never taken shortcuts. I know how to clean cat litter. Oh, and my 'uppity attitude' and 'lax standards' are no longer acceptable for Dr. Tammy."

"What?" Aunt Sally's voice reminded Reed of a red-tailed hawk screeching. "She's had it out to get you ever since she started dating that cocky vet. It's her problem you dated him first. Well, all I can say is she can have him. You've put up with her long enough."

Reed wheeled closer to the table. Interesting.

Claire raised her hands to the sky. "When I think of all the degrading things she's put me through. For her to fire me? She'd better not bad-mouth me around town the way Mark did, or so help me—" She noticed Reed then. "Oh, hi. Sorry. Having some drama here."

He hadn't been this entertained in some time. He flourished his hand for her to continue. "Don't let me stop you."

"I'll make you a plate and you can tell me everything." Sally scurried inside as Claire dropped her head into her hands.

"Sorry about your job."

"Thanks." Claire straightened. "I tried hard to make her happy, hoping she would see my effort. To get fired was a shock."

Reed tensed. She wasn't going to cry, was she? He didn't do well with emotions, especially not tears. He scoured his brain for something to say to lighten the mood. "I can call some Chicago hit guys to rough her up. Say the word."

The hint of a smile crossed her lips. "You'd do that?"

"Sure. I'm bored out of my mind anyhow."

She let out a sigh full of despair. "What am I going to do now?"

"The zoo, right? Isn't that the plan?"

She rubbed her forehead. "I hope so. The applications have been pouring in, though. What if I don't get it?"

"You'll get it."

Tilting her head, she leveled a stare at him. "What if I don't?"

"I can put in a word with your dad," he teased. "He owns several car dealerships, right?"

Claire made a gagging gesture. "Never. I worked there as a teen. I'd rather bus tables at Pat's Diner."

She slumped again, looking as lost as a baby kitten without a mother. And the sight scrambled his head, made him think things he normally wouldn't. Before he knew it, he opened his mouth. "Go online, see who else is hiring and fill out applications. In the meantime, you can drive me around town to take pictures for estimates."

Hope lit her magnificent eyes. Too much hope. He swallowed. Painfully.

"You're right. I'll find a job. And if we could get estimates, Uncle Joe's would open sooner. But..." She frowned, defeated once more, and stared at the table. "Aren't you going back to Chicago in a few days?"

Reed had planned on it until this moment. His head yelled to get out of Lake Endwell while the getting was good. His heart, on the other hand...

"Nah, I kind of like this cottage. I'll be on crutches soon, and I'm dying to go fishing. And I don't want some hack builder talking the store owners into cheap remodelings. The downtown needs to maintain its historical integrity."

"I worried about that too." Claire picked at her nails. "Maybe I'm being unrealistic, but I want the downtown to look the way it always has."

Reed nodded. "I know a few firms who would make sure they get it right. It's not as if I have to be back to work. Not for almost a month anyway."

"I'll do whatever I can to help." Her face glowed, the

desperation he'd witnessed earlier completely erased. She covered his hand with hers. "Thank you."

Awareness hit him. And dread.

This woman was dead set on giving him a superhero complex.

And he'd never been a hero. Didn't have the qualifications.

He prayed he could escape before she found out.

Chapter Five

A knock on the door caught Claire off guard. The clock said half past nine in the morning. Who would be coming over this early on a Saturday? Not Reed. He couldn't get up her porch steps in the wheelchair. Not Libby. She liked to sleep in, the later the better. And not her brothers—summer drove them out of the house at dawn to fish. Claire waited for whoever it was to come in, but...

Another knock.

Her black calf-length yoga pants, faded lime tank top and makeup-free face weren't what she would wear for visitors. What if it was the eighty-year-old woman four cottages over who liked to stop by—Yorkie in hand—and stay for hours?

Claire cringed. Not the Yorkie. Not the hours of chatting. She opened the door a crack.

Reed stood on her porch. He lifted his eyebrows as if to say "surprise."

Her mouth dropped open and she did a double take. He was out of his wheelchair!

"You're on crutches!" She clapped, her nose crinkling. "Get in here. Tell me what happened. Did you have a doctor's appointment this morning or something?"

"Nah, I have one Monday. Dale brought these over for me. Thought I'd want to try them."

"But Dad isn't a doctor. You could hurt your leg more. I don't think this is a good idea."

"So this is it, huh? Your private lair." He pushed past her and thunked his way through the entrance to the sectional couch in front of her picture window. His heather-gray T-shirt had a Bears logo on it, and black basketball shorts skimmed his knees. "Don't worry. I'm being careful."

"My brothers have handed me that line too many times, Reed. I know better." She waited to assist if he needed it. "At least stretch your leg out. This couch was made for lounging."

"I plan on it." He moved the crutches to the side, lowered his body to the couch and reclined back, satisfaction all over his face. "Ah."

"Happy?"

"Yes," he said. "You have no idea. I couldn't take the chair of death another minute."

"The wheelchair was that bad?"

"Worse."

She chuckled, moving around the couch to prop a pillow under his foot. "Did anyone bring you breakfast?"

"Your dad. Ham-and-cheese omelet, toast and Sally's strawberry jam." He brought his hands behind his head.

"Dad didn't bring me any breakfast," she said. "I'll have to have a chat with him."

"Face it, he likes me better." His playful grin, tanned face and warm brown eyes flipped her stomach.

She launched a pillow at him. "Actually, I think you might be right. It's been ages since he brought me breakfast."

"Watch the leg, there."

"Oh, I'm sorry. Did I hurt you?" She had no sooner finished speaking than the pillow hit her square in the face. She glared. "Playing dirty, I see. Using my sympathy against me."

"I have to use any weapons I can." His grin lit up his face, and her breath caught. This teasing should feel familiar since she had grown up with three brothers, but teasing Reed? Entirely too…everything. Extra elements mixed. Attraction. Excitement. Awareness.

"Uh-huh." She flicked her fingernails. "I'm glad to see you're in less pain.

Reed studied the walls then the bookshelves. Claire assessed her house from his point of view. The white television cabinet contrasted with the pistachio walls, and she'd hung framed photos of her family next to black-and-white pictures of animals in the wild. Did he find it as cozy as she did?

"Nice place," Reed said with an appreciative stare. "It's…you."

"Thanks. I couldn't imagine living anywhere but here."

"It's mellow, comfortable. I could sit here all day. Actually, I might." He folded his hands on his abdomen. "Hope you don't have plans."

He wanted to stay? All day? No objections on her part.

"How long have you lived here?" he asked.

"Five years," she said. "I bought it from Dad after college."

"Bought it?"

"Yeah, when you have as many brothers and sisters as I do, things get ugly if anything isn't fair. We all agreed me buying the place was the best way to keep the peace. Dad set aside money for each of us to go to college, but I earned a full-ride scholarship. He insisted I take the money anyway, so it became my down payment. I got a great deal on my favorite cottage, the family had someone to keep an eye on Granddad and the Fourth of July always, always gets celebrated next door."

"Independence Day. It's not a small affair for your family, is it?"

She raised one knee to her chest and rested her chin on it. "Got that right. All the Sheffields and Perceys gather together. It's a good time. You can't miss it."

He shook his head. "I'll leave the fun for the Sheffields and Perceys. By the way, who are the Perceys?"

"My mom's side," she said. "A smaller bunch, but still a ton of laughs."

"Do you ever get—" he drew his eyebrows together "—sick of being surrounded by family?"

"What?" She scoffed. "No. Never."

"Huh."

A subject had been heavy on her mind lately, but she didn't know how to bring it up. Maybe being blunt was the answer. "Has your dad been over yet?"

His cheekbones strained against his face. "No."

"I could drive you over there." Why it bothered her that his dad wasn't around, she couldn't say. She knew Roger. A nice man. Quiet, but always friendly when Jake brought him and Barbara to family functions. So the fact that Roger and Reed didn't talk made no sense.

The set of Reed's jaw assured her he didn't want to discuss it. A squeaking noise from the backyard made Claire hop up. "Do you know what you need?"

"A long nap?"

"Nope."

"Do I want to know?"

"You need to meet my otters."

He grimaced. "I'm not much of an otter person."

"Everyone is an otter person. They are the cutest things. Just wait." She loped to the back sliding door. Could he get down the three wide stairs using his crutches? Shouldn't pose a problem. Then she returned. "If you can't make it down to the lawn, I'll bring them to you."

"I can make it." He slowly pushed himself up.

Opening the fridge, she searched for the hard-boiled eggs she'd shelled yesterday. The Ziploc baggie hid behind a jumbo bottle of vanilla-flavored coffee creamer. "Come on. You're going to love them."

Out in the sunshine, she waited for Reed to clear the door before closing it. He handled the steps easily and settled into one of her lounge chairs. She blew out a low whistle.

Hansel and Gretel raced her way, and Claire held an egg. Gretel bounced over, sniffing and raising herself on her back legs before snatching it out of her hand. Then she squeaked. Hansel followed suit.

Claire grinned at Reed's paralyzed expression. "You can pet them. They're lovable. Go ahead."

Reed tentatively lowered his hand. Gretel sniffed it and bumped his palm with the top of her head. "Uh, Claire? What do I do?"

"She's asking you to pet her."

His lips curled down, but he patted the top of her head. "She's soft."

"Gretel has a velvety coat. Hansel's is a bit rougher, but you probably wouldn't notice."

"Hansel and Gretel? Fairy tales, huh? I didn't realize you were into happily-ever-after and all that."

"Hardly." She sniffed. Much like in the Disney movies she grew up on, when Mom died, life got complicated. As much as she wanted to believe in happily-ever-after, she hadn't seen much evidence of it. "Fairy tales look great on paper. In real life, not so much."

"Cynical." He stroked the otter's fur until it raced away to the tall grasses by the fence. "I wouldn't have thought that of you either."

"Why not?" She wasn't cynical. She was realistic.

Reed rubbed his chin. "You're…well…you seem happy. When you're not losing your job."

She laughed. Yesterday afternoon she'd helped Reed create a spreadsheet, and she'd personally contacted the owner of JoJo's Jewelry as well as several other store owners. Most wanted to work with Reed, which pleased her to no end. The loss of her job stung less now that she was helping him and the town.

"Um," Reed said. "What are they doing?"

Gretel burrowed into a patch of tall grass, and Hansel dove on her. They flipped and flopped, nipping at each other's necks, and made more squeaking noises. "Oh, they're playing. That's how they bond."

"Aren't you worried they'll hurt each other? I see teeth."

Claire laughed, shaking her head. "No, if one gets too rough, the other lets him know. It won't be long and they'll curl up together behind the log." She leaned forward, pointing at a small woodpile. "See how it's close to the low wall of rocks? Their favorite spot."

Reed studied the rest of the yard. "Do you have a dog?"

"No," she said. "Only the otters for now."

"Do your brothers have a dog?"

"Why?" Did he like dogs or something?

"Isn't it obvious?" He made a point of staring at the assortment of squeaky toys, small stuffed balls and ropes strewn around the yard.

"Oh, the toys." She chuckled. "They're for the otters. They get bored, so I keep different things on hand. Like the pond over there." She gestured to the water feature. "It's deep enough for them to improve their swimming skills, but not too deep. The logs provide natural napping spots. The trees, shrubs and grasses give them things to hide in, but they still like playing with toys."

He stretched his neck to see where she pointed. "Did you put the pond in for the otters?"

"No, Dad and I installed it two years ago. I originally thought I might keep turtles back here, so I oversized it and added a deeper section. I'm glad I did. It's funny how God works. I planned on having turtles, but He knew two baby otters needed the backyard more."

"I don't know. You're saying God knew all along you'd be taking in otters? That's the real reason you put the pond in? What about your turtles? Aren't you mad your plan changed?"

Claire considered before answering. "Sure, I like turtles, but these little guys mean so much to me. I want to work at the zoo so badly. Then I can see them every day. It's going to be hard giving them up. Everyone told me not to get too attached, but I'll be honest, detachment isn't my strong suit."

The otters dove in with a splash. After paddling awhile, they floated on their backs.

Claire tapped Reed's arm. "Watch. Sometimes Hansel will take Gretel's hand. It's adorable." Reed squinted at the pond. When one reached for the other's hand, Claire lifted her shoulders, let out a laugh and smiled at Reed. "See?"

"I can't believe it." His eyes widened. "They really are holding hands."

"They're besties."

The intensity in Reed's expression sent a waterfall of bubbles from her throat to the bottom of her stomach. While everyone who stopped by thought the otters were charming, she was ridiculously pleased Reed thought so too. Maybe it was because he'd shown the most skepticism about them.

"Who is your bestie?" Reed asked in a low voice.

She sank back into the chair and cocked her head to the side. "Good question." She had lots of friends. But a best friend?

"Who do you go to when you're having a bad day?" Reed added.

Put that way...

"Well, I get great advice from Aunt Sally. And if I need help with a project or fixing something, I call Dad. Libby makes me laugh. My brothers show everyone a good time." But even as she talked, she frowned. She didn't have a go-to person to share everything with.

"What about you?" she asked. "Who is your best friend?"

"I have a few buddies from work." His gaze glued to a cloud floating by.

"Good buddies? Or work buddies?"

"John, my boss, is probably my closest friend. He's not afraid to tell me the truth. Plus, he's always believed in me. I like to prove him right."

"You'll be the best vice president the company has ever had." Which reminded her…she had to stop feeding the attraction. He had a promotion to get to, and she had to nail the zoo job, help plan Libby's wedding and make sure the otters enjoyed a smooth transition to their new home next month. A commotion from the deck had her whipping her head back.

"Hey, there you are." Tommy and Bryan clomped down the steps. "We brought lunch." Bryan held up two packages of hot dogs. "I'm firing up the grill."

"Hot dogs? It's ten-thirty in the morning." Claire peered over her shoulder. "How many fish did you catch?"

"Don't ask." Tommy opened the grill and pushed the ignition button. At six feet tall, he was solid with wide shoulders and dark hair. Ninety-eight percent of the single, nonrelated females in the county hoped he'd give them a second look, but ever since his split from Stephanie a few years ago, he'd kept women at a distance. "What's wrong with this thing?"

"Ugh." Claire smacked her forehead. "The igniter broke. You need to light it with a match." She bounded up the steps, slid the screen door open and grabbed a box of matches. "Where's Sam?"

"Locked in the library to finish his paper. I can fix it." Bryan yanked the box from her hand. Two years older than her, he had lighter features than Tommy, but he was handsome too. His dark blue eyes gave him a brooding air.

"Hey, Reed." Tommy held up a can of soda. "We're putting a picnic-slash-volleyball-game together. Claire, Aunt Sally told us to drag you there if we had to, but you're going to the picnic. She said, and I quote, 'Claire spends too much time at home. She needs to have some fun.'"

Claire cringed. What a lovely impression for Reed to have of her. An otter-loving recluse.

"Actually," Reed said, "I wanted Claire to drive me into town to take pictures of the damage. It will help us figure out the best companies for the jobs."

Help get Lake Endwell back on its feet, or be pestered by her brothers all afternoon? Taking pictures with Reed was the clear winner.

"Stop here." Reed pointed to the damaged warehouse outside town. The roof peeled back like a can of sardines, and the parking lot was littered with materials flung from the storm. "Was this business on the list?"

Claire parked as close as possible, avoiding boxes and beams. "I'm not sure. Let me check." He caught a whiff of the coconut scent of her lotion. Big mistake. The tropical delight diverted his attention from the pulse in her neck. That little throb mesmerized him too.

Focus.

"So, did you find it?" Reed opened the passenger door, but his crutches were in the backseat of her ancient vehicle. He waited.

She flipped through the legal pad. Took her pen and slid it down until she found the name. "Yes. We called them. They've already contacted their insurance company as well as two commercial builders, and they don't need help."

Reed slammed his door shut again. "Great. Let's continue into town, then."

Claire weaved the four-door car through the debris back onto the road. "Three of the freestanding stores downtown don't need us either. They called Dad yesterday and told him the adjuster stopped by. They have a list of leads to call about the work."

"At least some of the businesses are seeing progress."

Claire slowed as they neared town. "Yeah, but those three use the same insurance company. The others haven't had the same success."

Reed could attest to that. He'd called most of the insurance providers Dale gave him. Some were motivated to rebuild. Others dragged their feet.

"There's got to be something we can do to get moving on this." Claire pulled into a parking spot on the edge of town. "I'm frustrated. Isn't that what insurance is for? To get you back on your feet quickly?"

"Wait. Repeat what you just said." Reed glanced at her profile. Indignant looked cute on her. And her words had pricked an idea, but he couldn't grasp hold of it.

"To get them back on their feet?" She lowered her chin, staring up at him from under her lids.

"No, not that. The other part."

"There's got to be something we can do."

"That's it." He opened his palms and turned to her. "Exactly. We need to shift the power." He let the possibilities wash over him. Yes. "You're brilliant, Claire."

Her cheeks grew pink, but she shook her head. "Brilliant. Sure."

"No, really. What we need is to get the remaining insurance companies and all the builders motivated. And I know how we can do it."

"How?"

"We need an event. Media. Tell the insurance companies and the construction firms we're honoring all of them in a special celebration for the rebirth of Lake Endwell. We'll put a time limit on it, so they'll have to get the work done before then. They wouldn't want to look bad to the papers, magazines and television crews."

Claire gasped, her smile reaching across her face. "Yes! It's just what we need!" Then her face fell. "I wish we could do something for the people who didn't have home owners' insurance."

"What if we include a fund-raiser to pay for their repairs?"

"Yes!" She beamed. "A 5-K. And a bake sale. Oh, Uncle Joe might host a benefit dinner if we can get his restaurant reopened."

Reed guessed she was right. The Sheffields were the most generous people he knew.

"Let's talk while we take pictures. It's stifling in here." He tugged on his collar and opened his door. "Have you considered buying a newer car? One with air?"

"I ride my bike almost everywhere. I don't need a new car. Wait for me to come around with the crutches."

Reed waited. Didn't want to. But he did. This week had taught him several things, one being that his leg hurt a lot less when he did things Claire's way.

She handed him a crutch.

"Thanks. Why don't you take pictures with my phone?"

"Okay." She helped him with the other crutch and kicked the passenger door shut. "I have the list too. We can mark the addresses as we go."

He wasn't used to the crutches, but he found his stride quickly. They had to walk in the street, since the sidewalks held mounds of concrete and bricks. Dumpsters were arriving on Monday.

"Eerie, isn't it?" He hitched his chin across the street. "How that side looks like it didn't see the storm, but this side is full of rubble."

Claire tucked the legal pad under her arm and snapped pictures. "It is creepy. I guess I should be thankful some of the town was spared. It would be hard to be an owner on this side, though. Wouldn't you be wondering, 'Why me?'"

Kind of like how he felt when he woke up in the hospital. "Yes. I would."

They continued up Main Street.

"After this, let's head over to the restaurant," Reed said. "I want to see it for myself."

When she didn't answer right away, he stopped walking. "What's wrong?"

"Can Dad take you tomorrow?" She didn't meet his eyes, and her tone sounded strained.

"Why not today?"

"Well, Jake and Libby are coming to the cottage for dinner, and I don't know if we'll have time."

He checked his watch. Dinner was hours away. Was she avoiding the restaurant?

She skipped ahead, then turned to face him. "Smile."

He gave her his best "are you kidding me?" stare.

"I'll take the picture anyway," she warned. She clicked. "That wasn't so hard."

He lunged forward to catch her, but someone called his name. He searched the area to see where it came from. A silver Volkswagen crawled to a stop next to him.

"When did you get on crutches?" Barbara had rolled her window down. Dad pulled the car parallel to Reed.

"Hi, Dad." Of course Dad would be driving through at this moment and kill the mood. Keeping his armpit on the crutch, Reed gave a little wave with his hand.

"Reed." Dad nodded and stared ahead.

"How are you feeling? Did you have a doctor appointment? Are you doing okay?" Barbara gushed, her eyes darting back and forth. Her fingers lifted to her pearls.

"Hi, Roger. Hi, Barbara." Claire sidled next to Reed, bent and waved to them. They both said hi.

Reed opened his mouth to answer some of Barbara's questions, but Dad beat him to it. "When are you going back to Chicago?"

He gripped the crutches and straightened. He hadn't seen his dad all week, and the first thing out of his mouth was to ask when he was leaving? He clenched his jaw. Didn't know how to respond without getting ugly or sarcastic or both.

Claire leaned her forearm on Barbara's open window ledge. "He's staying awhile to help us get the town back in shape. Isn't it great?"

"Wonderful, Reed." Barbara smiled, but worries raced in her eyes.

"Don't worry, Dad. It's only for a few weeks. Then I'll be out of here."

Chapter Six

Libby, Jake and Reed sat with Claire around the cottage table a few hours later. Claire looked up from her plate. A heron landed near the shoreline. The huge windows showcased the endless blue of lake and sky. The bird stood immobile, ready to catch dinner. Speaking of food, she'd forgotten to fill her salad bowl. Garlic mingled with the aroma of grilled steaks.

"We're thinking Labor Day." Jake passed the salad to Claire.

"Why Labor Day?" Claire scooped lettuce onto her plate and eyeballed the dressing options.

"Summer wedding," Libby said. Her flirty white sundress revealed tanned shoulders and arms. Claire had to give it to her sister—the girl always looked stylish.

"It depends if the church is free that weekend." Jake crooked his finger for Reed to pass him the bread basket. "I'm guessing Monday."

Libby frowned, setting her fork down. "Not Labor Day, Jake. Labor Day weekend."

He slathered butter on a roll. "Friday and Saturday— you know they're probably booked. Monday is the logical day."

"No one gets married on a Monday." Libby's voice rose.

"No one but us." His mouth split into a toothy grin as he playfully tugged Libby's hair. A brief smile graced her face.

Claire glanced at Reed, who gave her a "what can you do?" shrug. Yes, what could she do? She sensed a showdown brewing, and she wasn't in the mood for it. Ever since they'd run into Reed's parents earlier, Reed had been quiet. No more playful banter. They'd taken pictures of the buildings methodically, and every idea Claire shared about the possible town event was met with a mumble or a nod. Not that she blamed Reed. His dad hadn't picked the best time to ask when he was going home.

"Mondays are the most hated day of the week." Libby pierced a piece of meat onto her fork. "I want the right time and place." Her expression dimmed. "Exactly one week ago, we'd have been eating our wedding dinner. We should be married now."

"I know," Jake said. "But it happened, and we can't do anything about it. Stop dwelling on it."

"Stop dwelling on it?" She sniffed. "A tornado ruined our wedding. I will not stop dwelling on it."

"We'll have a new date. Labor Day."

She gave him a dark look. A very dark look. "Classes start back up then. I can't skip the first week of school for our honeymoon."

"Talk to your teachers. They'll understand."

"Easy for you to say."

The back-and-forth accelerated, and Claire pressed her fingers against her temples. This conversation would not end well. When Libby sank her teeth into a subject, she didn't let go. And Jake was being just as stubborn.

"Libby," Claire said in her brightest tone. "Why don't you help me with dessert?"

"I'm not done eating dinner." Libby glowered at her. "And I'm not getting married on Labor Day."

Jake and Reed focused on their steaks. Smart men. The ice cream needed to thaw for easier scooping, so Claire escaped to the kitchen. She'd already heard enough of Libby's arguments this week. Couldn't they compromise and move on?

Claire opened the freezer, grabbed the mint-chocolate-chip ice cream and set it on the counter to soften. She heard Reed say, "Tell me the date, and I'll be there for it."

She braced both hands on the counter. Ever since Reed had agreed to stay the rest of the month, she kept forgetting he wasn't staying for good. And the more time she spent with him, the more she wanted him to stay.

She must be vulnerable. From the tornado. And losing her job. And because he was taking the time to help people get back on their feet, she'd put him on a pedestal.

God, help me protect my heart better. I've got a nasty habit of throwing it to the wrong guys. And Reed is the wrong guy. He's got a vice president position waiting for him. I've waited years for this zoo position to open up. I'm not losing it again.

Claire took a deep breath and returned to the silent table where no one made eye contact with each other. Wonderful.

"I haven't been down to the dock." Reed pushed his plate back. "Want to put a pole in the water, Jake?"

"Sure." Jake piled silverware on his empty plate and took Reed's too.

"You ladies joining us?" Reed's gaze met Claire's. Was he being polite or was that an invitation? His light brown eyes glowed. Invitation. An electric sensation skittered over her skin.

The wrong guy.

If she kept telling herself that, maybe her body would agree.

"No, you two go on ahead." Libby waved them on. "We're avoiding the mosquitoes."

Claire sighed. Sitting on the dock with her feet in the water sounded way better than listening to the inevitable rant Libby had prepared. Reed clopped his crutches to the patio door. A blast of heat warred with the air conditioner but lost the battle when Jake closed the door behind them.

"Can you get over him?" Libby scooped the silverware and marched to the sink. "Like I should drop my classes and jump up and down about getting married on Labor Day. A holiday, no less. Who gets married on a Monday? A Monday?"

"Want me to call Pastor Thomas and find out what dates are available the rest of the summer?"

"No, I'll take care of it." Libby leaned her backside against the counter, anxiety twitching in her pale blue eyes. "I have this bad feeling."

"What's wrong?" Claire put the ice cream back in the freezer and quickly filled the dishwasher. She washed her hands, then waved to Libby. They retreated to the living room. Libby, twirling a piece of hair between her fingers, sat on one end of the couch and faced Claire at the other end. "What kind of bad feeling?"

"I'm not sure. Maybe this is all a mistake. I mean, Jake's getting on my last nerve, which, let me tell you, is a very frayed nerve."

Claire's lips twitched. Her sister might be melodramatic, but she was funny too.

"He's not being considerate of my feelings at all," Libby said. "I want a Saturday wedding. A summer wedding. A honeymoon when I'm not taking classes. Why is that so hard for him to grasp?"

One of Claire's feet dangled to the floor, and she hugged the other knee to her chest. "If you want Uncle Joe and

Aunt Sally to cater the reception, you might have to be a little flexible."

"And I don't appreciate his suggestion we go to the Upper Peninsula for our honeymoon. Our original plan of driving to Maine was bad enough."

"What's wrong with Maine?" Claire asked.

"Nothing, if you love riding in the car for fifteen hours. Yeah, a road trip is *not* my definition of romance, but even that beats camping in the UP. I wanted to fly to Aruba, Cancún—Florida, even—but no-o-o, he's being a total cheapskate."

"Camping could be romantic."

"Sure, Claire." Libby huffed. "Real romantic. I melt with delight at the smell of OFF! bug spray. And the shower situation up there—well, it's probably best described as rustic. I'm shuddering at the thought."

"He isn't thinking of tent camping. Is he?" Claire shivered, grimacing. Her sister—the one who spent at least thirty minutes straightening her hair every day—in a tent?

"He wants to borrow his dad's trailer." She whirled her index finger in circles. "Yippee. Talk about romantic."

"Jake has student loans up the wazoo. I'm sure he doesn't want you starting your marriage deep in debt."

"I don't want to start my marriage covered in ticks." Libby flicked her wrist. "What's the big deal? This is a once-in-a-lifetime day."

Claire bit back her reply. The phrase "once in a lifetime" had been uttered twice before with Tommy and Bryan, and they both regretted spending wads of money on weddings when their marriages didn't last. "Sounds like you're having cold feet."

"Cold?" Libby shook her head and rubbed her forearms. "No. Chilly maybe. I'm really starting to wonder."

"About what?"

"Maybe God *was* telling me something. With the tornado and all. You keep saying we're young, and I still say I'm old enough to make my own decisions, but what if the tornado was a sign? What if I'm marrying the wrong man?"

"Wait a minute, Libs." Claire held out her hand. "I never thought you were marrying the wrong man. I just wanted to be sure you're ready for that level of commitment. You saw how it was with our brothers."

Libby rolled her eyes. "I'm different."

"Marriage is forever."

"I know," Libby said. "That's why I'm not sure Jake is my forever."

"What makes you think he isn't the right guy?"

"If he's being this high-handed now, what will he be like in five years? I think I should have some say in our life."

Claire stretched her knee back out. "Absolutely. Marriage is a partnership, not a dictatorship. But God made men and women different for a reason."

"Exactly. Maybe Jake and I are too different. His idea of a perfect wedding doesn't come close to mine. I'm not settling."

Claire's spirits sank. Did Libby consider marrying Jake *settling*? "That sounds unrealistic."

"Why?" Libby's eyes widened.

"Nothing's perfect. What's wrong with what Jake wants?"

"Everything. Haven't you been listening? A Monday wedding. Road trip. Bug spray." Libby grimaced. "A wedding should be more about what the bride wants."

"A wedding is the first day of the rest of your life as a couple. Compromise a little."

She sighed. "Fine. I'll think about the dates again, but I hate the idea of a Monday wedding. I mean, would you get married on Labor Day?"

"I don't see myself married." Claire snorted. As if she

ever thought about herself and marriage in the same breath. "You'll figure it out."

Libby launched into a plan for new invitations. Claire had heard all she ever wanted to about wedding invitations. In fact, the hours she'd put in planning her siblings' big days should qualify her for an honorary degree in wedding planning. Getting all caught up in the details? She grimaced. Eloping was the way to go.

Not that she would have the opportunity.

God had blessed her with many things. Her family, her cottage, her otters and now a chance at her dream job. She had enough.

Her gaze strayed to the windows. Jake sat in a folding chair next to Reed. Their fishing rods angled over the water. They looked peaceful, content. The back of Reed's head reminded her of the silky feel of his hair that night in the storm.

She averted her eyes.

Yes, her life was enough.

Reed slowly cranked his line. "Jake, can I ask you something?"

"Go for it."

"Does it bother you I'm staying a few more weeks?"

"What?" Jake shook his head. "No way, man. I like having you here. I'm glad you're staying longer. This cottage sits empty most of the time anyway."

Reed dug through the tackle box for a different lure. Jake had stopped by twice during the week and texted often. It meant more to Reed than his brother could know.

The bobber floated in rhythm with the gentle waves. Either algae reeked or Reed did—his shirt stuck to his body from the humidity. The inside of his cast was probably breeding fungus at the speed of light.

"You going to reschedule the big Alaskan adventure?"

Jake asked. "It's killing you not to be there right now, isn't it?"

"This leg is killing me more than anything, but it is hard to let go of the idea. I looked forward to it for a long time." Reed grinned. "I don't see me planning it again. I won't have time once I slip into the VP position."

"I'm glad you got promoted, but I was hoping...well, you're always busy and the new position will probably take even more time. At least you're here now." Jake finished attaching a new lure. "Have you talked to Mom and Dad lately?"

Frowning, Reed rubbed his chin.

"What was that look for?" Jake asked.

"Nothing."

"Come on, you're mad about something."

Reed didn't want to have this conversation, but the lazy lake, the geese flying overhead and the sticky heat must have lulled him. Dad hadn't stopped by this week. Not once. But Barbara called constantly. Reed couldn't take much more of her perkiness. "Sure."

"Sure?" Jake gave him a penetrating look. "That sounds like no to me."

"Dad and I haven't had a normal conversation since I was a kid."

"But he talks about you."

Dad talked about him? Yeah, right.

"You have eyes, Jake. Have you ever seen Dad and me hang out, relax?"

"That's Dad," Jake scoffed. "He's quiet."

"It's more than quiet."

"He's not social, but it doesn't mean anything."

"He hasn't talked to me, really talked to me, since my mom died."

Jake yanked the pole. "No one ever talks about it. I don't even know her name."

"Meredith."

Jake nodded.

"Everything changed after her funeral." Reed checked his bait. Half a worm remained. He attached a different lure and recast.

"Look, I'm sorry," Jake said. "I shouldn't have mentioned it."

"No one talks about it because…" Reed focused ahead. "She was drunk. Her car split the tree in half."

Although technically he wasn't to blame for his mom's death, guilt still found a way of creeping in. The tension between him and Dad traced back to that day. Reed braced himself for the pain of the past to swim back. His grandmother's hard eyes. The whispers in the school hallway. "I heard her neck snapped in two" and "My dad said she smelled like a liquor store." Reed clenched his jaw. Why did the past still reduce him to a seven-year-old kid?

Tiny ripples broke the clear surface of the water. "Jake?"

"Yeah?" Jake set the fishing rod to the side.

"Thanks."

"For what?"

"Checking on me. Coming over tonight."

"Are you kidding? I wish you'd move here so we could hang out more."

What Reed wouldn't give to live near his brother. He'd always loved him, even when Jake was a gap-toothed kid. Bought him candy every Friday, gave him piggyback rides and played catch in the backyard. Jake brought a sense of normal back to Reed's life even with the strain between him and Dad. After high school Reed shouldn't have abandoned him—but losing his best friend and the home he'd known for ten years had left Reed confused and angry.

"You can always move to Chicago." Reed nudged his shoulder.

"Not likely, no offense." Jake chuckled, jerking his chin

toward the cabin. "Libby and I want to raise a family here. That is, if we get this wedding back on track. I don't know what her deal is. One minute she's dying to marry me. The next she acts like the tornado was my fault."

"You're brave." Reed trained his gaze on the lake.

"Brave?" Jake snorted. "Why? Marrying Libby?"

"Marrying at all."

"Nah, I love her. We're meant to be together. She'll come around. Labor Day will work fine. She'll see."

"I hope so." Reed might not know much about love, but Libby didn't seem the budging type.

The give-and-take Reed could do. The forever aspect— a shiver rippled over his skin. He would like to offer a woman forever with him, but how could he be sure she would keep her end of the deal? Or that he wouldn't accidentally destroy what they built together?

He couldn't.

And he needed to remember that.

During dinner he'd stared at Claire too long and too often. But she'd been tense—he'd seen it in her pursed lips. The lips drew his attention. He'd averted his eyes only to latch on to the graceful lines of her neck. When he spent this morning at her cabin, he'd been filled with peace. Even those otters made sense, and he was not an animal person unless it barked. Then Claire's enthusiasm over planning the town celebration had been contagious. Made him forget he wasn't staying, that he'd worked seventy-hour weeks for eight years to get this promotion in Rockbend Construction, that small towns—family towns—didn't work for him.

His stupid mind kept coming back to the same questions. What would it be like to hold Claire? To get close enough to feel the warmth of her skin? To kiss her?

Haven't I learned anything? Every time I've trusted

someone enough to let them see who I am, they reject me. I always end up with nothing.

He would leave marriage to Jake.

Chapter Seven

"We're all set to fix the sun porch at Miss Gert's this afternoon." Dad sprinkled hot sauce over his eggs. "The boys will be there around one. Can you get her and the cat out of the house for a while?"

"I'll think of something." Claire sipped her coffee at Pat's Diner after church the next day. "Maybe I could drive them to my place. Tell her I'll give Whiskers a free checkup."

Dad shook his head. "She probably won't go for that. Hates doctors."

"True." Claire glanced at Reed, who sat next to her in the booth, his cast protruding slightly in the aisle. She'd peeked at him all morning. Before church. During church. After church. And now here. The man should not be allowed to wear a dress shirt. Especially not one rolled up at the sleeves, revealing muscled forearms.

Reed cut into his farmer's omelet. "She'd come over for Sally's pie. Anyone would."

Claire nibbled on a slice of bacon. Good point. Sally baked a mean blueberry pie. "If Aunt Sally's willing to bake, I'll lure Miss Gert and Whiskers to my house with treats."

Claire wiped her hand on her napkin and started in

on her pancakes while Reed and Dad resumed their conversation about the restoration. Dad, naturally, threw out
ideas left and right.

"Three months is unrealistic. Most of the historic buildings will need nine months to a year before they'll be ready
to open again." Reed took a drink of black coffee. "The
damaged houses should be ready this fall."

Dad's expression turned thoughtful. "The point is to
get things moving. To motivate everyone involved. A year
seems too far out."

"I know, but I've been doing this a long time. It's wrong
to give people false impressions. These are big, complicated jobs, and to do them right takes time."

A waitress stopped by and topped off their mugs.

Claire poured two sugar packets into hers and stirred.
"Setting the celebration date for a year from now wouldn't
necessarily mean we couldn't build a buzz about it. In the
meantime, we could chart the progress on a big board in
the town square and start some of the fund-raising we
discussed."

Dad's eyes lit up. "I'm sure Joe would want to host that
benefit dinner you mentioned. I'll ask him this afternoon."
He stabbed a sausage link, cut a piece and shoved it in his
mouth. "Maybe I'll just text him now before I forget." He
grabbed his phone.

Claire met Reed's eyes, smiled and shrugged. Dad
wasn't one to linger or think about something too long.
She leaned in and said quietly, "He likes to jump in with
both feet."

"I noticed." His breath warmed her cheek. Sitting next
to him had not been the smartest move she'd ever made.
His aftershave—the ocean-fresh smell she'd come to
anticipate—had teased her all morning.

"Yep." Dad set his phone back on the table, a satisfied
smile on his lips. "Joe wants to throw a benefit dinner at

the restaurant when it reopens. You don't think it will take a year too, do you, Reed?"

"No. From what the contractor told me, I'm guessing it will be reopened soon. A month? Two tops."

Dad attacked his breakfast again. "Why will the buildings downtown take so long?"

"A company will assess if they need new foundations. I'm assuming they will. Then you're basically looking at renovating five new stores per block simultaneously. And they'll all need to be modernized. If the damaged areas are severe, sections might need to be rebuilt. One problem, though, has been bothering me."

"What?" Claire and Dad said at the same time. They glanced at each other and laughed.

"The insurance will pay for replacement costs, which will cover basics, but the budget might not cover architectural details like the special doors or elaborate windows ruined in the tornado."

Claire's eyebrows drew together. The improved stores Reed described sounded nothing like Lake Endwell. "But they'll be ugly. Tourists come in the summer for the cute factor—the historic charm."

"I know." Reed nodded. "I've got some ideas, but they'll cost money."

Dad pushed his plate to the side and folded his hands on the table. "What are they?"

Reed turned his coffee cup twice before answering, "Hire a construction firm from Grand Rapids specializing in historically accurate restorations with modern features. All new wiring, efficient furnaces, energy-saving windows. I've seen their work. They do things right."

Dad took a big gulp of his coffee.

"Why do you say that with hesitation?" Claire shifted to watch Reed.

"It's expensive. The store owners will have to come up

with whatever insurance won't cover. I have a few ideas how to get around it, but…"

"What kinds of ideas?" Claire asked. Reed's serious expression was even more attractive than his teasing smile. She bit the inside of her lip.

"A visit to the mayor and city council might help. If the town could kick in some of the money—"

"We could raise the rest." Dad slapped the table. "I like it! Sheffield Auto will make a contribution. Others will too. Tell me about the materials this company would use."

As Reed and Dad discussed beams, dimensions and rebar—whatever that was—Claire finished her breakfast. Part of her wanted to plant a kiss on Reed's cheek for his willingness to help solve the town's problems. The other part? Wanted out of this booth to clear her head. Sometimes God's plans seemed terribly clear, and other times she had no clue.

It was obvious God sent Reed here to help rebuild Lake Endwell. No locals had the kinds of contacts and experience he did. But she didn't necessarily believe God sent Reed here for her to lose her heart over. She was familiar enough with attraction to admit she had it bad. She'd gone down this road before—with Justin. And it had led her to bad decisions.

But good had come from it. She truly understood her purpose in life after breaking up with Justin and crawling back to Lake Endwell.

Her family. The summer she moved to Atlanta? The Sheffields fell apart. Newlyweds Bryan and Abby fought constantly, Tommy and Stephanie split up, Sam partied too hard with the wrong crowd right after his high school graduation and Libby failed her driver's test. Twice. If Claire had been around instead of working at a dog kennel six states away…

When she moved back and bought the cabin, she'd immediately thrown herself into the lives of her siblings. She took Libby driving every night after work. Checked on Tommy throughout the day. Flat-out told Sam he'd better get his act together or he'd lose his scholarship. And Bryan—sweet Bryan—she'd given him hugs and ice cream as much as he'd let her. He'd married the wrong woman. Not much Claire could do there.

Slowly, life got back to normal. She'd even started dating again. And when Mark treated her as if she were beneath him, complaining about her casual clothes, grumbling about her close relationship with her family and expecting her to wait around when he had other plans, she'd dumped him. Been strong. Told herself she deserved more.

"...next Memorial Day would be a good date for the celebration. If we can talk to the mayor and store owners and get a plan together, they can hire the firm and get a schedule in place."

Claire took a sip of her lukewarm coffee. Her purpose hadn't changed. But Reed poked at memories. Dreams of a husband and babies and being surrounded by her loved ones. Listening to him—his take-charge attitude, his vast knowledge of construction—she felt it was clear he belonged in a high power position. In Chicago.

Lake Endwell had him for a few weeks. But what did it have to offer him beyond that?

Nothing.

Assisting Reed gave her something good to do while out of work, but she'd be wise to remember this was temporary. She'd moved away once, and everything fell apart. Now she finally had a chance to fight for the job she'd turned down years ago. Some people seemed to have it all, but Claire had never been one of them. The zoo job and her family were her top priorities. Not romance. Not Reed.

"What do you say, Claire?" Reed asked. "Should we set up a meeting with the mayor and city council?"

"Yes. Definitely." Her head cranked out ideas to protect her heart. "But I'm only available afternoons. I decided to volunteer at the zoo every morning." There. She wouldn't spend every waking minute with Reed.

"My work at the dealerships can be done anytime." Dad pointed to her. "Claire, if you work with Reed in the afternoons, I'll help out in the mornings."

"Dale, you and I can make phone calls and go through my checklists. Tomorrow we're getting crews out to the restaurant. I don't care what it takes." Reed turned to Claire, an appreciative gleam in his eyes. "And when you get back from the zoo, we'll drive to job sites."

Every afternoon in her tiny car with Reed? Her pulse skyrocketed. Maybe she should've volunteered all day, every day at the zoo.

Too late now. Her summer just got interesting.

The following Friday morning Reed stood in front of the large closet and debated over what shirt to wear. Dale had laundered all Reed's clothes yesterday and dropped them off earlier. Strange to have Claire's dad volunteering for this stuff. Not that Reed minded. Every day Dale brought breakfast and brewed a pot of coffee, and they went through the checklists, determined what calls to make and tied up the busy work.

Yeah, Reed liked his mornings with Dale.

Afternoons with Claire, on the other hand...

Exhilarating, but dangerous.

No matter how many times he told himself to stay focused on the work, he failed. It would start with her pointing out a historical detail about an abandoned barn on the outskirts of town, and before he knew it, he was caught up in her enthusiasm. Teasing her when they made the rounds. Answering her intelligent questions after a meeting with a contractor. Staring into her pretty eyes. Eating dinner with her on the cottage deck. Talking about nothing until the sun went down.

He set his crutch against the wall and pushed the hangers to the side in search of a shirt.

So he had a thing for Claire. It wasn't that big a deal. And, technically, he and Claire were conducting business.

They'd met with Mayor Brantley Tuesday afternoon. The mayor called an emergency city council meeting on Wednesday, and after a lot of back and forth, they agreed to consider a multifaceted plan to pay for the historically accurate buildings. Claire had been a big part of getting them to consider it. When council members asked Reed about the construction firm, he shared technical details, but Claire was the one who explained how those details would benefit Lake Endwell.

Next up? A town meeting. The community would be able to have their say since it would involve taxpayer money. As for the big media event to celebrate the town's reconstruction, city council had approved the date—next Memorial Day. Meanwhile, Reed had contacted the firm from Grand Rapids he had in mind, and yesterday they came out to start working on their bid.

Yes, Lake Endwell was on the road to recovery.

A dark gray polo shirt caught Reed's eye as his cell phone rang.

"Hey, John, what's up?" Reed pulled the shirt from the hanger and hobbled to stand near the window. Two blue jays flew around a cedar tree.

"Remember the addition to the hospital in Denver we bid on last year?"

"If I remember correctly, they put an indefinite hold on the project." Reed tossed the shirt on the bed.

"They're moving forward with it. I'm having Cranston update the numbers. They want us to fly out July 15 for a meeting."

Reed frowned. Less than three weeks from now. The days were passing quickly. "Great." Reed kept his tone firm. "Book the flight. I should be out of this cast by then, so after we tour the hospital, we can determine the best team to get it done."

"Good to hear your enthusiasm, Reed. I can always count on you. Can't wait to have you back."

They said goodbye, and Reed took a seat on the edge of the bed.

John *had* always been able to count on him. And vice versa. It was one of the few relationships that worked in Reed's life. But he didn't want to fly away from Lake Endwell yet. And this wasn't just because helping restore the town energized him, or the fact that he got to see Jake every other day. Part of it was Claire. She'd become a good friend. The girl he couldn't stop thinking about.

Every night, he and Claire shared childhood stories, their college experiences—she commuted and got scholarships; he lived in the dorm and took out loans—the latest movies, books they'd read and the best music. They'd talked about faith—and he found himself drawn to her quiet spirituality. She was a doer. Someone who lived her faith without preaching it.

Admirable.

Claire had made his time in Lake Endwell fun, and tonight he was returning the favor. They'd worked hard all week. Now it was time to relax. Sally had assured him Claire spent Friday nights at home on the couch.

Not if he had something to say about it.

"Hello? Reed? It's Sally." Her voice traveled down the hallway.

"Be right out." Reed hastily grabbed the shirt. Privacy wasn't high on the Sheffields' priority list. Balancing on one leg, he shoved his arms in the polo and clip-clopped his way on the crutches to the living room.

"Well, you sure are looking handsome." Sally glanced up from the counter. Tiny baseballs swung from her ears. "How's life in the cast treating you today?"

The corner of his mouth kicked up. "Not bad, but my leg is shrinking. It itches like crazy."

"Hang in there. It's normal."

His cell phone rang. He checked the caller and opted not to answer.

"Aren't you going to get that?" Sally lifted a container of food out of the bag and smelled it.

"It's Barbara. I'll call her back."

"But she'll be worried." Her "you'd better answer the phone" stare forced him to grit his teeth, but he made no move to answer it until Sally put a hand on her hip.

He refrained from raising his eyes to the ceiling. "Reed here."

"Oh, you're there. It's Barbara. How are you doing? Do you need me to pick you up for any appointments? Or I could keep you company if you want. I have a five-hundred-piece puzzle. Should I bring it over?"

"Uh, no, thanks." He flicked a glance at Sally, rummaging through his fridge, setting cans of soda on the counter. Drinks for his date—well, nondate—his *surprise outing* with Claire. "I have plans tonight."

"You do?"

"I appreciate the thought, though." He clicked his teeth together. All this time with the Sheffields made him think about patching things up with his own family. "Is Dad around?"

"He's at work. I can give him a call to stop by, though. Did you need him?"

Yeah, he needed him. The years kept sprinting by, and Reed pretended he didn't need anyone, but his time here hammered home the facts. He hadn't tried to heal the rift with his father. And he wanted to.

"No, no," Reed said. "Just thought I'd say hi if he was around."

"Well, I'll be sure to tell him for you, and I'll have him call you later too."

"Okay." He pressed End and set the phone on the table. Barbara had told Reed four other times his dad would call him later. Dad never called.

Sally breezed to the table and wiped her hands. She slapped a chair for him to join her. "I have everything you need for dinner. Claire is going to love it. You're good for her. She's living for herself a little more now you're here."

He frowned. "But she's been spending all her free time helping me and volunteering at the zoo."

"Pfft. She loves the zoo. And working with you isn't hard. I'm sure there's a herd of girls back in Chicago who would trade places with Claire in a minute."

A herd? Like cattle?

"Too bad I couldn't find the cooler." Sally craned her neck toward the kitchen. "I'll have to bring mine over."

"That's okay. There's got to be one here somewhere."

She narrowed her eyes. "It would only take me a minute to run home and get it."

"Really, I'll find one."

She opened her mouth, then shut it and smiled, patting his arm. "Sorry, hon, I know you're independent. I just have to be sure my boys are comfortable, you know."

My boys? Reed's throat froze—Sally considered him one of her boys?

Why does she include me? And why does Barbara make an effort? At what point will they realize I'm not worth the trouble?

"If you don't find the cooler, you give me a call," Sally said. "I can't thank you enough for staying and helping us out."

"It's nothing."

"It's not nothing. You put your life on hold and made all those calls. Joe and I can't believe how quickly the work is getting done." She tapped her red fingernails on the wooden table.

"Making phone calls is part of my job."

"But this isn't your job, and we've been making the same calls and getting nowhere. You actually got them to listen. You love your work, don't you? You must be missing Chicago."

A blow-off remark perched on the tip of his tongue, but *my boys* echoed. "Yeah."

"We're growing on you, aren't we?" She arched her eyebrows. "Sure wish you lived around here, but Lake Endwell doesn't offer the same opportunities as Chicago. I get it."

He almost protested.

Lake Endwell offered more.

No.

He couldn't be vice president *and* live in Lake Endwell. And whenever he opened his heart a crack, it got filled in with concrete. Mom. Her family. Collin. His family.

He didn't think he could handle losing Claire and her family too.

Chapter Eight

What a crummy Friday.

All week Claire had spent extra hours at the zoo, hoping to impress the zoo director, Tina Atley, enough to increase her chances of getting the position. But it had been almost two weeks since Claire had submitted her application, and Tina hadn't called yet. Shouldn't someone have contacted her by now for an interview?

Claire stomped to the refrigerator for a Diet Coke. No silver cans, not in the usual spot next to the half gallon of milk or hiding behind the head of cauliflower she meant to cut up. Brown spots spread like dirty fingerprints across the white florets. She should probably throw it away.

Slamming the fridge shut, she headed to her bedroom to change.

The worst part about the day? Claire ran into one of the zookeepers and found out the latest news. News she didn't like. Not one bit.

A second cousin of Tina's recently graduated with a degree as a veterinarian technician and wanted the position too. Second cousins had a nasty way of taking priority over experienced applicants.

Claire pressed both palms on her dresser top and glared at her reflection in the mirror. Frizzies escaped her ponytail, her mascara smudged the corner of her left eye and the sunburn she'd gotten on her nose last weekend had started to peel.

Maybe she should go to bed.

If someone else got the zoo job, she wouldn't be able to take care of the otters after they left her house. How could she hand over their care to some stranger?

And where would she work? She couldn't imagine a job not animal related. The two vets in town both hated her, and they'd both fired her. Fantastic.

She'd have to look for a job in the city. She'd have to start over.

Pulling out a pair of stretched-out shorts and an over-size, stained white T-shirt, she changed. A knock on the door had her smoothing her hair.

"I have a surprise for you." In a charcoal polo shirt and cargo shorts, Reed stole her breath. His smile highlighted the crinkles around his eyes. She couldn't look away from his lips. Of course the hottest guy in the county would show up when she wore her scrubbiest clothes.

She swiped a finger under her left eye in an attempt to erase the mascara smudge. "What kind of surprise?"

"A good surprise."

"Can it take a rain check?"

"No. It can't." His smile faded.

Claire brushed her toe back and forth and fingered the edge of the T-shirt. "I appreciate the gesture, but I—"

"You don't know what the gesture is," he said, the twinkle in his eyes returning. "So how can you appreciate it?"

Claire exhaled loudly. "I had a really bad day."

"Then you definitely need this. Come on."

What did he have planned? Her silly heart leapt for joy, but logic yelled, "Slow down." The time they'd spent together all week? Amazing. Reed got things done. And he didn't act like a big shot. He asked her about the job sites they checked, wanted to hear about the owners and included her in every meeting.

He was slowly opening up to her. No guy made her laugh the way he did.

But that was the problem. They weren't just working together. They were swapping stories every night. The more time they spent together, the more she liked him.

She already liked him a little too much.

But he would be leaving soon. And that "but" was a big deal. It would be hard enough to say goodbye without getting even more attached.

Reed cleared his throat. His eyes pleaded with her for… something. He needed her; she sensed it. And caved.

"You win," she said.

"My favorite words."

She couldn't help it, she chuckled.

"Meet me on the dock in ten minutes," he said. "You didn't have plans tonight, did you?"

Not unless pigging out on Ben & Jerry's and watching reruns of *Dr. G: Medical Examiner* counted as plans. "No, I'm free."

"Good. Bring a sweatshirt."

She returned to her bedroom, threw on shorts showcasing her toned legs and shoved her arms into her cutest black tank top with My Monkey Made Me Do It scrawled below a cartoon monkey face. A quick retouch of her makeup, her favorite sandals, a hoodie around her waist and she was ready to go.

It had rained the night before, so she hopped over the puddles in the drive separating her property from Granddad's. The fishy scent of earthworms made her smile.

Home. It smelled like home.

Reed beat her down to the dock and pushed the pontoon door open with his crutches. Claire held her breath.

He wasn't getting on the boat by himself, was he? Didn't the fool know he could slip and hurt his leg even worse?

He handled the transition easily, glanced up and waved. "Your chariot awaits."

"Looks like Dad's pontoon to me." She picked up her pace to join him.

His tanned face and mussed hair reminded her of a photo shoot, one with a title something like "Rich people yachting." Her heart flip-flopped. He winked. "I have an apology to make."

"For what?"

"I have to put you to work. Could you get the stuff over there?" He lifted his crutches. "I don't trust my ability to get on the boat with these things *and* carry food."

Aunt Sally's unmistakable takeout bag perched on top of the picnic table. Claire hauled the blanket, bag and cooler onto the pontoon.

"Ready to set sail?" He flashed a mouthful of white teeth.

Her lips twitched. "It's not exactly sailing."

"Pretend it's a sailboat tonight." He nodded to the monkey. "Nice shirt. The monkey made me do it too. We're off on an adventure. A culinary adventure if Sally has anything to do with it. Now hold on, this could get bumpy."

"Do you want me to drive?" She followed him and stood behind the captain's chair, inches from his cropped hair. Wanted to run her fingers through it.

"What kind of question is that? Of course not. Your dad gave me a crash course this morning. I could use some help untying the ropes, though."

"Crash course, huh? I hope you don't mean it literally." She unlooped the ropes keeping the boat docked.

"Ready?" He waggled his eyebrows. "I've been eyeing this baby since I got here. You take the seat next to me. I've got this."

She obeyed, biting her tongue when the boat bumped against the edge of the dock.

"No worries," he said. "I can handle it."

It lurched at an angle, and Claire covered her mouth to stifle a giggle.

"Are you laughing at me?" He steered the craft to open water. "I should play the injured card and remind you of my broken leg. You would feel guilty then, wouldn't you?"

"Oh, yes." She nodded solemnly. "I would be eaten up inside."

"I knew it."

They sped to the west. The roaring engine and spraying mist prevented conversation. Ah… She leaned back. Water, nature, trees. Her favorite escape. After a tour of the lake, they rounded a bend and Reed slowed the boat. "Is this a good spot?"

"For what?" she asked.

"For dinner. I'm starving."

"Yes." The bend provided privacy. Tall maples, cedars and pines formed a semicircle around them, and four cottages dotted the opposite shore. An eagle soared above, outlined against the cottony puff of a cloud. The scent of fresh lake water wreathed to her nose.

"I'll drop the anchor." Claire made her way to the back.

"I'll watch."

Heat rose to her cheeks. *He'll watch?* Reed had shed his defenses all week. While she liked how he teased her, she didn't like how it made her senses churn.

She hadn't been keyed up over a guy in a long time, and now? Her senses misfired, her pulse tripped, her skin prickled.

She couldn't afford the physical chaos. Romance and attraction didn't last. If she let her feelings run free, she'd be the loser. Reed wasn't staying. And neither of them wanted forever.

Did she?

Did it matter?

She hoisted the anchor and dropped it in the water, where it slipped below the surface and disappeared.

Reed couldn't tear his gaze from Claire across from him on the other cushioned bench. Her tanned arms and legs revealed her sporty side, but her bright pink toenails gave away her feminine style. He stole a peek at her matching lips.

He and Claire had discussed the progress on various buildings in town while they ate turkey subs and pasta salad. After dinner, he sprawled on one bench and she took the other. Now the silence made him think things. Things he was better off not thinking about.

Like pink toenails and slim ankles. Wisps of dark hair lifting in the breeze. The slight curve of a shoulder.

"So, uh," he said, then shook his head. Great. Nervous high school kids had nothing on him. "What was so bad about today?"

"Hmm?"

"Earlier. You mentioned a bad day."

Her eyes hid behind large black sunglasses. Sighing, she barely moved. "There's another strong contender for the zoo position."

"Who?"

She sat up and moved her legs to face him. "Tina's second cousin."

"Ah." Sympathy swept in.

"Family trumps experience, you know. Oh, and I stopped in at Lake Endwell's garden club meeting this afternoon. I had the fund-raising sign designed, so I showed them the mock-up and asked if I could install it in front of the gazebo at City Park. Well, they told me yes, but the sign's colors sparked a big argument about petunias versus geraniums. Ugh. Why can't everyone agree?"

He grinned. "Welcome to my world. One of the first things I learned as project manager was to present a set number of choices for my clients. It's easier on everyone." He hitched his chin to her. "How did the sign turn out?"

"I love the sign. It's big, bold. Should be ready in a week. I hope it motivates everyone to work together for the sake of the town." She rubbed her biceps. "Speaking of not compromising, Libby called earlier. She nixed the backyard barbecue reception idea. Back to square one."

"Jake hasn't been much better, Claire. Some of the suggestions he's made have made even me cringe. And I'm not into weddings."

Neither spoke as dragonflies flitted from lily pads to the edge of the pontoon. A light gust of wind made a faint swishing sound. Relaxing.

"Can I ask you something?" Reed's cast still extended on the cushions, but he dropped his other foot. He'd learned a lot about Claire this week, but one question kept popping up, one he'd been unwilling to ask until now.

"Sure." Her shoulders lifted slightly.

"When we first met, you said you lost your dream job and wouldn't leave Lake Endwell again. What happened?"

"You went for the biggie, didn't you? Couldn't have asked me something easy, like why I'm such a terrible cook." Her lopsided smile teased. "The story is pretty simple. I fell in love my final semester of college. Justin took a job in Atlanta. I was offered a position at the zoo here, and even though everyone told me not to, I turned it down and followed him. Rented a tiny apartment two blocks away from his. It didn't end well."

"This is Lake Endwell, though." He couldn't help himself.

"Ha-ha." With a fake glare, she propped her sunglasses on top of her head.

"Hey, I didn't name the place." He put his hands up in mock defense. "Don't get mad at me."

"Actually, the Native Americans or the French most likely named it. We think it means Lake Star. The Ojibwe word for star is *anang*, and the French word is *une étoile*. Blend the sounds *on* and *twah*, mix it with a little English and it sounds like *end well*. A lot of the towns, rivers and lakes were named by a blend of French and Native American words."

He recognized a stalling tactic when he heard one, but he enjoyed the animation playing across her face. "Interesting."

"It is, isn't it?" She settled back against the cushions.

"But it doesn't explain why it didn't end well."

Still reclining, she waved a hand in the air. "He kept blowing me off, not coming over. Didn't take long for me to track him down in a bar with his hands all over some clothing-deficient party girl. He said, 'I knew you'd be good and wait for me, Claire. You've always been my Tuesday girl.'" She let out a disgusted half laugh, half grunt. "A Tuesday girl."

"What a jerk." Mixed emotions roared through him. He wanted to throttle the idiot, but he also wanted to hold Claire's face in his hands, look her in the eye and tell her he would never hurt her. The back of his neck bristled. He couldn't promise her that. Reed fisted his hands. "Must be the world's biggest moron."

"Thanks." A tiny, sad smile lifted her lips. "When I moved back home, the zoo position had been filled, my siblings' lives were falling apart and I didn't want to live with my dad. So I prayed. Bought the cabin, helped my brothers and sisters get back on their feet and promised myself I'd never, ever move away again. My life's purpose is here."

"What is it? Your life's purpose?" He couldn't help himself. Did he have one of those?

"I've always been the one my brothers and sisters lean on for support. I didn't fully appreciate it until I left." She shrugged. "Besides, I've said it before—I want a man to put me first. The last guy I dated was Mark, the other vet here in town. He started off okay but proved to be as selfish as Justin."

"What category would you put me in?"

A genuine smile spread across her face. "Not selfish. Not one bit. You've done so much to help our town. We're all grateful. I'm grateful."

He nodded, his heart strangely heavy. Her honesty pressed against his chest. Made him want to reveal more. "I'm good at my job. I'm not good at the other stuff."

"What other stuff?"

"Long-term. Getting close."

"Why do you say that?"

He stared at the tree line. "It's obvious I'm not tight with my family, Claire. And I might never be. My dad sees my dead mom whenever he looks at me."

She coughed. "Wh-what?"

"He and I don't talk, barely make an effort with each other because of it."

"Did he say that?"

He flicked a bug off his cast. "Didn't have to."

"Then how do you know?"

He rubbed his chin then met her gaze. "My mom crashed her car into a tree. She was drunk at the time. After the funeral, my whole life changed. We moved within a year. Dad met Barbara, and he avoided me." He raised his eyes to the sky and shook his head. "I resented Barbara. She made him happy, made him laugh, and I couldn't even get him to hug me good-night."

Claire crossed over and kneeled in front of him. "Oh, Reed. I'm so sorry. My heart hurts for you. I wondered why your dad hasn't come over."

He brushed his thumb over her cheek. "It's not worth your heart hurting. I'm not cut out for this family stuff."

"You were a child. A little boy. You didn't do anything wrong."

"It's not just that. I practically lived with my best friend in high school. His parents treated me like I was their son. I finally felt wanted again, like I belonged somewhere. We went on family trips. You name it. They washed their hands of me too."

"Why?"

"Doesn't matter."

"It does to me."

"I like you. A lot." He rested his hand on her shoulder. "And if my past was different, I would be asking you out right now. I'm glad I could be here to help get the town back on its feet, but as soon as the store owners downtown decide on a construction firm, they'll have a new project manager. I'll be heading back to Chicago in a few weeks."

The sun's rays grew longer and less powerful as waves gently lapped at the boat. "I like you too, Reed, and I know you have to leave. But before you go, don't you want to try to work things out with your dad? Maybe it would change the way you feel."

"I don't know."

"Just think about it. And no matter what happens, I hope you and I will remain friends."

Her tropical scent teased his nostrils, and the understanding in her eyes made him want one thing—to feel, for one brief moment, what it would be like to be more than friends with Claire. He shifted and cupped her chin, never breaking eye contact. She moistened her lips.

He took it as an invitation.

Splaying his fingers in her luxurious hair, he slowly dropped his lips to hers. She tasted…better than he had imagined. Like happiness. Like Claire. He pressed her close to him, vaguely aware her arms had wrapped around him. His chest tightened as he savored her softness.

She was steady, unwavering.

And he drank her in.

Finally, he broke off the kiss, keeping his face next to hers. His breath came in raggedy intervals. Playing around with unwavering steadiness wasn't an option. He could try to work things out with Dad the way she suggested, but it wouldn't change the fact that he wasn't cut out for closeness, nor would it change his mind about the vice president position.

He dared not look in her eyes. A man only had so much willpower, and Claire had blown it away without so much as a poof. "We'd better get back."

Two more weeks. He needed to get back to real life. Needed to return to Chicago before Claire cut through all his defenses.

Chapter Nine

Avoiding Reed all day yesterday had proved harder than Claire thought.

Like now, instead of enjoying the lazy Sunday afternoon, Claire still couldn't get her mind off Reed's kiss. Libby's chatter wasn't helping.

"And Jake was okay with Pastor Thomas officiating the ceremony Friday night before Labor Day, but I'm not sure how many people could make it…" Libby lounged in a periwinkle-blue Adirondack chair facing the pond. Gretel bounded her way, but Libby snatched her hand back. "Eww, what's it doing, Claire?"

"She's being friendly, Libs. Pet her."

Libby tentatively patted Gretel on the head. "There." The otter sat up on its hind legs and poked its nose in the air. "Now what?"

Claire rolled her eyes and tossed a baby carrot. Gretel left Libby alone.

"Where were we? Oh, right. So the food situation might not work…" Libby launched in on wedding planning. Claire tried to pay attention, but Reed's kiss blew her intentions away like dandelion seeds. Concentration? Impossible.

All his talk about not getting close to families only unleashed her desire to have him here, where she could include him. Everyone deserved a family. Who did he turn to when life threw garbage his way? Who did he rely on in situations like the one he was in now—broken leg, physically vulnerable? The Sheffields could be his family.

Her stomach dipped and she placed a hand over her abdomen. Why was she mentally forcing Reed into her family when he didn't want one? She would not pursue the fire lit by his kiss. Sure, he was the most amazing guy she'd ever met. But she'd thought the same about Justin. And this— this sizzle between her and Reed—wasn't a commitment. It was proximity. Working together. A summer flirtation.

Claire watched Hansel chase Gretel around the yard until they stopped next to her chair. She stroked their backs, laughing when they rolled over and ran off.

"Are you even listening to me?" Libby waved her hand in front of Claire's face.

"Sorry. Got a lot on my mind. Keep going."

Libby launched into the wedding scenarios again, and this time Claire paid attention. When she finished the update, Libby hugged her. "Thanks, Claire. I don't know what I would do if I couldn't talk to you about all this. I'd lose my mind. Jake gets all tense and cloudy eyed when I mention setting a new date. I get the feeling he couldn't care less."

"He's a guy. They're not as excited about the plans." Claire walked her to the back gate. "He wants to be married to you. He loves you."

Libby flashed a smile and left. Claire flopped back into her chair as her phone rang.

"I'm sorry to call on a Sunday." Tina's voice rang strong. "But I found out the otter exhibit won't be open on time. The cement needs to be repoured. Is there any way you could keep the otters an extra week?"

Claire inhaled and counted to three. As much as she loved Hansel and Gretel, she didn't love the position she was in. She toyed with telling Tina yes, she would keep the otters *if* promised the permanent job.

"Don't you like them?" Tina asked in her blunt manner.

"I love the otters. Of course I want to take care of them. I'm a little worried I won't be given the opportunity to continue working with them when they move to the zoo."

"You'll always be able to work with them. You've been volunteering with us for years. That's not an issue."

Claire didn't want volunteer work. She wanted to be on the zoo payroll. Wanted to work with the otters every day. Did Tina understand how important the job was to her?

"Claire, if you can't do it, tell me now. I'll have to make arrangements."

The battle between getting what she wanted and doing what was best for the otters pressed against her skull, giving her a dull headache.

"You don't have to make arrangements," Claire finally said, a weight dropping in her stomach. "They can stay with me."

"Thank you. We appreciate it. We'll get them moved into the quarantine area after the other otters are settled into the exhibit. Sorry to inconvenience you."

"It's not an inconvenience. They're thriving here."

"Good. Good. This will be less disruptive for them. Let me know if they need anything. Thanks again."

She said goodbye and hung up.

Lord, forgive me for my selfishness. I should be grateful for the opportunity to care for these otters, and all I can think about are my own wants. How I want the job. How I want to be their permanent caretaker. How I want Reed to stay. Help me humble myself to do Your will.

A breeze swished through the trees. Was it okay to want more?

No. It wasn't okay. She should be content. She should be happy with her life.

Help me trust You, Lord.

She'd trusted before. Trusted the idea of love, of dreams, of her prince charming.

Trusting in big dreams was hard.

The phone rang again. "Hello?"

"I realized we haven't set up an interview time." Tina's voice boomed. "How does Wednesday work for you?"

"Wednesday is perfect." The gloom disappeared. Cheer spread through her body. Maybe one of her dreams would come true. *Thanks for giving me hope, Lord.*

She flew to the gate, ready to run to Reed's and tell him. But she stopped, hand on the latch. How would she get him off her mind if she kept racing over there every five minutes?

The sizzle would never fizzle if she didn't at least try to keep some distance.

Three minutes later, Claire crossed the driveway and strolled along Reed's lawn. Distance was good and all, but the man lived next door.

With a clipboard in hand, Reed sat in a camping chair on the end of Granddad's dock. Slipping out of her flip-flops, she lowered her body and let her feet drop into the water. "Reports?"

His eyes gleamed. Was he happy to see her? She rested her hands behind her and lazily swung her legs. The water cooled her ankles, reminding her of childhood worries about what swam below. Minnows? Sharks? Rare sea creatures?

"Nah," he said, flipping a sheet of paper over. "I'm trying to figure out if we missed a store. The east side of Main Street should have ten total spots to rebuild, but I only have nine owners listed."

Lifting her dripping feet back on the dock, she stood and crossed to Reed. Peering over his shoulder, she studied the digital mock-up of the street the building commissioner sent him. Her cheek almost touched his hair.

"There." She pointed to the third spot. "This looks like two separate stores, but it's really one. Ripley & Sons Hardware occupies both. Dad bought me the ugliest winter boots there when I was nine. I cried all night. He wouldn't return them."

"Boots?" Reed raised one eyebrow. "From a hardware store?"

"I know, right? Big, brown and heinous." Claire dragged another chair over to sit next to Reed. "Have you talked to Mike Ripley? The hardware store always felt choppy. Maybe they can redesign it to be more open."

He tapped the paper with his pen. "I'm assuming they merged two existing stores. Didn't they tear down the divider wall?"

She scrunched her nose, unsure how to describe it. "There wasn't a wall, but there were big square columns all over the place and the floor wasn't level. You stepped down in spots. Felt like a fun house at the fair."

"Ah, I understand. I'll give him a call."

"Guess what?" She raised her hands near her shoulders. "I have an interview with Tina for the zoo job!"

"That's great, Claire. It wouldn't surprise me if she hired you on the spot."

"I hope so." She reached over to playfully swat at his shoulder but held back, feeling awkward all of a sudden as she remembered their kiss. She didn't want him to think she'd read more into it than he intended.

Two Jet Skis zoomed past, water spraying high behind them. What now? She couldn't think of anything to say. Discussing town business and the zoo? Easy. But what he'd revealed the other night about his dad kept replaying in her mind. "Reed? About the other night—"

"I'm not apologizing for kissing you." His eyes burned through her, and the feel of his lips on hers roared back.

"I'm not either."

"Good."

She sighed. "I think you should talk to your dad."

The muscle in Reed's cheek flickered. "No."

"Hmm," she murmured. "Do you want to go over there? I can take you."

"Nah."

"You're here. Don't you want to reach out to him? See if anything more is possible?"

He stared out at the lake.

"What do you say we swing by your dad's house and invite him and Barbara out for ice cream."

"I don't know."

"One cone, Reed. Then we'll leave."

Taking his time, he finally said, "If I agree, then you have to do something for me."

Her pulse bolted. "What?"

"You still haven't been to the restaurant since the tornado."

"I've been busy." Claire wasn't sure she wanted to. The fear from that night still flooded her brain occasionally.

"You're not busy now."

She didn't speak.

"Why haven't you been there?" he asked.

"I don't know." She crossed one leg over the other. "Uncle Joe's place has a special spot in my heart."

"Is something else going on? Are you afraid another link to your mom will disappear?"

She hadn't really thought about it, but he had a point. "Maybe. What if I go back and instead of holding onto the great memories, I relive the roof wrenching off and being trapped there for hours? I'm a little scared to see the restaurant all torn up. I think I've spent more time there than my own house."

"You don't have to relive anything. The tornado is over." His tender smile eased the tension in her shoulders. "It's torn up, but in a good way. You come with me to the restaurant, and I'll tag along to JJ's for ice cream with Dad and Barbara."

"JJ's? No way. We're going to Tastee Freeze."

He grinned. "I had a feeling you'd say that. Restaurant. Then Tastee Freeze. Deal?"

Dread lingered in the pit of her stomach, but she nodded. "Deal."

They slowly made their way up the dock. Claire pulled her car around for Reed.

Ten minutes later, she parked at Uncle Joe's Restaurant. From the outside, it appeared the same as ever, but the Dumpster, stacks of lumber and heavy equipment on the side of the parking lot reminded her otherwise.

"I have the code to the side door. Come on." Reed swung his crutches to the newly constructed addition, already covered in gray siding, and he opened the door, holding it for Claire to enter.

With jittery nerves, she went inside. Drywall covered the framed walls, buckets and tools dotted the plywood floor and electrical wires stuck out here and there.

"Wow." She moved forward, taking in all the details, then pivoted to Reed. "You did all this?"

"Me?" His warm gaze held her hostage. "No. I gathered crews from all over the county. Their hard work did all this."

Claire closed the gap between them. "I can't believe how much got done. And so quickly. All because of you."

Reed tucked her hair behind her ear. "It would have gotten done with or without me, Claire."

She gulped, shaking her head. "No, it wouldn't. Uncle

Joe couldn't get anyone out here to even give him an esti-
mate, let alone find anyone to do the work. You—you don't
know how much this means to them. To me."

His hand dropped back to his crutch, and he blinked.
"It's nothing."

"It's everything," she said. "How can I thank you?"

He lowered his head. "You don't need to."

She disagreed. Instead of terror or fear, she felt hope
and thankfulness. Reaching up on her toes, she wrapped
her arms around his neck and gave him a hug.

"So?" He cleared his throat. "Are you glad you came?"

"Yes." Claire took his hand and turned to the door. "And
now we'd better get that ice cream."

Reed let Claire take the lead and knock on Dad's door.
Barbara appeared, her face breaking into a smile at the
sight of them. "What a nice surprise!"

"We're getting ice cream," Claire said. "You two want
to come with us?"

"Of course we do!" Barbara ushered them inside and
called to the back, "Roger, Reed and Claire are here. We're
all getting ice cream."

"What?" His muffled voice carried.

"Ice cream. Oh, you can't wear that ratty shirt. Change
into a nicer one." Barbara turned back to them with a big,
uneasy smile on her face. Reed knew the smile well. It was
her let's-pretend-everything-is-fine expression. "He'll just
be a minute. Have a seat."

Reed hadn't been here in years. He found excuses to skip
Christmas. How long had it been? Jake's high school graduation? Reed took in the oak floors, turning orange with
age, the dark green and maroon plaid furniture, the framed
prints of frilly porches. Traditional. Barbara's touches.

"Is this okay?" Dad entered, tucking a short-sleeve
button-down shirt into his jeans.

"Looks great." Claire nodded enthusiastically.

A long moment held like a water balloon being filled to the max.

"Shall we?" Reed gestured to the door.

And it burst. Barbara and Claire chatted happily about some church thing, and he and Dad did the usual. Nothing. Everyone filed out. Claire drove the four of them to Tastee Freeze where they stood in line at the outside window.

"Reed, I'm telling you straight up, the turtle sundae is the best in the state." Claire nudged him with her elbow.

"How can you be sure?" He flashed her a fake skeptical look. "I believe Bryan claimed JJ's has the best hot fudge."

"Bryan doesn't know what he's talking about. Roger, doesn't Tastee Freeze have the best sundaes?"

His dad flushed and a small twinkle lit his eyes. "I have to agree with Claire here, Reed."

Wait. Were they having a conversation?

Reed lifted his crutch to Barbara. "What do you think, Barbara? Should I trust these two biased ice cream aficionados? Tastee Freeze or JJ's?"

She let out a giggle—Barbara, giggling?—and touched her pearls. "Tastee Freeze does have the lemon custard I'm so fond of."

"Okay, Claire. I'll order the turtle sundae, but this means we'll have to go to JJ's soon so I can compare."

"You're on." Grinning, she pretended to dust off her shoulder. "And now prepare yourself for deliciousness."

After they ordered, they found an umbrella-covered table out front. They discussed the town's recovery, and Claire filled Dad and Barbara in on all Reed had done to help out.

"Claire, you might be right." Reed scooped another bite full of caramel and pecans on his spoon. "This is really good."

"Excuse me." Mr. Jay, a hobby store owner affected by

the tornado, approached. "Reed, Claire, would you mind if I ask you another question?" He glanced in apology at Dad and Barbara. "The company you contacted gave me a few design options, and I could use your advice."

"Sure." Reed hobbled to his feet and followed Claire and Mr. Jay to the car. Two large presentation boards with sketched plans sat in the backseat. Mr. Jay pulled them out. Claire accepted one and held it up to Reed.

"I like what they did with the floor plan on this one," she said. "It's so open and inviting."

Mr. Jay nodded. "But would it be too open? I'm worried about losing display space."

Reed gestured for Claire to show him the other plan. She held it up.

"Don't you love the storefront on this sketch?" Claire's face beamed. "Talk about charming."

Reed studied them. "Mr. Jay, what are you leaning toward?"

He tweaked his mustache. "Both. Wish I could merge the two. Tough decision."

"Actually, you can," Reed said. "Ask the project manager to use the outside of this one and the inside of that one."

"I can do that?" Mr. Jay pressed his glasses to the bridge of his nose.

"Absolutely," Reed said.

"I'm glad I talked to you. I've been going round and round about this for two days." Mr. Jay smiled. "If there's anything I can ever do for you…" He shook both Claire's and Reed's hands, then loaded the boards back in the car.

"We make a good team." Claire fell in next to Reed as they made their way back to the table.

A good team? He blanched. Collin always used to say that to him. They *had* been a good team. Until Collin betrayed him. "Yeah, well, our ice cream's probably melting."

He felt her quizzical glance, but he didn't look at her. Couldn't explain the mixed feelings assaulting him. He lowered his body to the bench and picked up his sundae.

"You sure know what you're doing," Dad said, keeping his gaze on the table.

A compliment from Dad? Reed almost jerked his head back in surprise. "Anyone with my experience would do the same."

Barbara took a dainty bite of her lemon custard. "Now, Reed, that's not true and you know it. It's generous of you."

Heat climbed up his neck. "Don't mention it."

Claire studied him. Her knowing expression drove him crazy—crazy enough to want to hold her hand, to kiss her again.

She turned to Barbara. "Did Jake tell you about Miss Gert's porch? I had to convince her to come to my house with me—and Whiskers. What an ordeal. She flat out refused. I didn't know what to do."

"How did you get her out of there?" Barbara was all ears.

"Promised her I had a special fur-ball treatment. And we bribed her with Aunt Sally's blueberry pie."

Barbara laughed. "Anyone could be bribed with her pie."

"I know, right?" Claire chuckled. "I wish it could salvage Libby and Jake's wedding plans. What a disaster."

They launched into a full-blown wedding drama while he and Dad focused on the ice cream. Thoughts jumbled in Reed's brain, questions grown stale as the years went by.

Hey, Dad, why haven't we spoken since Mom's death? Why haven't you looked me in the eye in over twenty years?

"Well, what do you think?" Dad asked.

Reed blanked. What did he think about what? Miss Gert? Jake's wedding plans? Twenty years of silence?

"Pretty good ice cream, isn't it?" Dad dipped his spoon back into his sundae.

"Yeah, Dad. It is." Ice cream. That was all Dad wanted to know. And it broke the crusty seal around Reed's heart. Ice cream was a good start. There hadn't been an awkward moment the entire visit. Maybe there was hope for them yet.

Chapter Ten

"City council will be electing a committee to organize the restoration celebration next Memorial Day." Mayor Brantley folded his hands, resting them on his massive oak desk Monday afternoon. "Claire, your dad already volunteered to be on it. He's contacting local media outlets."

"That doesn't surprise me." She smiled, glancing at Reed in the chair next to her. He'd dressed up for the meeting. The man could stop traffic in that button-down.

"We have a team working on the application for federal aid." The mayor frowned and adjusted a stack of papers. "It's doubtful we'll qualify. Believe it or not, our damage won't be considered severe enough. In the meantime, we're petitioning the state of Michigan to help defray the cleanup costs."

"Not severe enough?" Claire straightened her back, her good mood dissolving. "Have they seen our town? Half of it's leveled."

"I know. From what I've been told, though, the cleanup would need to cost close to twenty million dollars. I'm thankful our costs will be a fraction of that. And we have options. Donations and fund-raising make a big difference in disasters like this. Thank you both for your efforts."

Reed pulled his crutches from the floor and stood. "Thank you."

"If there's anything more we can do to help, let me know." Claire followed the mayor to the door, where he shook both their hands.

"Will do, Claire."

She and Reed walked in silence down the hallway to the door. "When the mayor mentioned the possibility of federal money, it was like a beam of hope. To find out we won't qualify is really tough to take."

"I know." Reed opened the glass door. Drizzle fell, leaving tiny beads of moisture on them. "I'm supposed to meet your dad at the restaurant. Mind dropping me off?"

"Sure." She started her car. "I'm heading to Aunt Sally's. I need to drown my sorrows in whatever she baked today."

Before she shifted into reverse, Reed covered her hand with his. "Hey, it's going to be okay. Everything is on track. The town will get rebuilt with or without government assistance."

She tried to smile. "Thanks. I needed to hear that."

"And don't worry about driving me around tomorrow. John emailed another report earlier. I need to review it."

Her spirits sank lower. "Okay."

Claire dropped Reed off and drove to Aunt Sally's, letting herself in through the side door. "Yoo-hoo, it's Claire." She poked through the living room and kitchen, but no one was home. She texted Aunt Sally and instantly got a reply. Sit tight. At grocery store. Be back in a minute.

Claire took the lid off the Tupperware on the counter. Chocolate cupcakes. Just what she needed. She peeled the wrapper off one.

"The wedding is off." Libby, red eyed and wearing a pale pink sundress with a cropped denim jacket and cowboy boots, slammed the side door, then dropped onto the bar stool next to Claire. "I am done with him. It's over."

Claire's heart thumped at Libby's clipped words. What would make Libby cancel the wedding now? It didn't make sense. And why had Aunt Sally picked this moment to be out at the grocery store?

Libby clicked her nails on the counter. Crossed one leg over the other, swung it quickly, then switched legs.

"What happened?" Claire asked, licking the frosting off her finger. Her sister in anger mode always churned her stomach, made Claire want to fix whatever bothered her.

Libby whipped her neck to the side and glared. "He is the most unbending human being I have ever come across in my life. I'm convinced if I marry him I will be miserable. Miserable!"

Claire inwardly groaned. She didn't want to sit through a session of let's-bash-Jake. He was a nice guy. Not perfect, but a good, solid, Christian man. "Want a water or a pop?"

"Like I can drink right now. Claire, please. Didn't you hear me? When I informed him we would have to move the wedding to five o'clock to accommodate the pastor, do you know what he said?" Libby stood and began pacing, the heels of her boots clapping on the hardwood floor. "Well? Do you?"

"Um…"

"He said, 'If the pastor can't do the seven o'clock time, maybe we should forget having a Friday wedding and get married at the courthouse.'"

The courthouse? Claire sputtered. Had Jake lost his mind? Libby would never consider anything but a church wedding or a religious ceremony. And, Claire had to admit, she wouldn't consider it either.

Reed's support this afternoon filled the loneliest corridor of her heart. Working with him, partnering with him made her feel understood, special. Why couldn't she get it through her head he had a promotion to return to?

"Well, you can guess what happened. We got in a massive fight. He started yelling. He never yells. I told him to calm down, if he would open his calendar, we could figure out a better time, and do you know what he told me? Do you?"

She didn't. And she didn't want to. Claire prayed for wisdom.

"He told me to grow up."

They faced each other. Libby, impossibly fresh and pretty, Claire in her striped blouse and black pants. Her heart ached for the beautiful woman her sister had become. How many times had she agonized over her little Libby? When Bree made fun of her hair in fourth grade. When Libby's sixth grade teacher decided she had an attitude problem. When a trio of mean girls spread lies about Libby her freshman year.

And now this.

Claire rose and held out her arms. A tense moment later, Libby fell apart, sobbing. Claire rubbed her back, wishing she could take away her pain, wishing she had the right words, but words wouldn't fix this. "I'm sorry, Libby."

Libby pulled away and dried her eyes with the backs of her hands. "I'm sorry too. I'm sorry I ever fell in love. I should have listened to you."

Claire ran her hand up and down Libby's upper arm. "Don't ever regret love."

"How can I not? You were right. Tommy thought Stephanie was the one, and, what, six months later they broke up? Or take Bryan. He and Abby were divorced, like, two weeks after their one-year anniversary. Love doesn't work in our family."

"Love works, Libby. It does. It's not easy."

Libby sniffled. "And what about you? Justin broke your heart. We all knew it. How many times have I heard you say you don't see yourself married? You got it right. I'm not going down that dismal road either."

Guilt ripped through Claire. She had never intended to shut her sister off to love and marriage.

"Listen, Libs—"

Libby ignored her. "My face must have given away how hurt I was, because he tried to apologize, but really, after that, what is there to say? I told him it was over. He can find someone else. Some grown-up who wants to get married *in a courthouse*. I'm sure they'll be perfect for each other."

"Hold on." Claire stretched her hands out. "I understand how you're feeling, I do. But what happened between me and Justin is nothing like the relationship you have with Jake."

Libby studied her fingernails.

"I mean it. Jake cares about you. I see it in his eyes. It's in the way he treats you." She averted her gaze. "Justin never treated me the way Jake treats you. You're like a princess to him."

"I don't feel like a princess. I'm working on my degree and I have a part-time job. I pull my weight."

"That's not what I meant. Jake—"

"I'm not going to stand here and listen to another lecture on marriage from you. It's normal to want a church wedding, okay? I should have known you'd blame me." She stalked out of the kitchen, down the hall, to the front door with Claire on her heels.

"I don't blame you. Your ceremony *should* be in the church." Claire lunged for Libby's arm, spinning her to stop. "But I don't want to see you throw away someone special over little wedding details."

She wrenched her arm free. "That's the problem. You see all the marriage details as little. Well, I don't. Getting married by Pastor Thomas means a lot to me. I've been dreaming about those details since I was three. Sorry. I'm not like you—I don't want to live my life alone."

Libby flung the door open and strutted to her car, her chin angled to the sky. Every word sliced through Claire as they repeated continuously in her head. She had thought Claire wanted to live alone. That she mocked her for wanting a church wedding. Of all the cruel things to say, Libby had found the one that hurt the most.

Claire returned to the kitchen and dropped her head in her hands.

She couldn't believe this had just happened. She'd been worried about Libby rushing into a lifelong commitment but never realized how she was coming across. Did Libby really think Claire was against marriage?

Lord, I don't know what to do. What can I say to get through to her?

She waited, listening, needing an answer. This was her sister—she couldn't afford to mess up any more than she already had. *Oh, Libby, why can't you see past your stubborn side?*

Should she apologize for giving Libby the wrong impression? Try to get Jake and Libby together to talk things out? Or…her throat grew tight—should she let them work it out on their own?

Everything within her shouted, *No!* She needed to fix this. Could she let her make her own mistakes? Libby wasn't a baby anymore. She'd figure out the right course for her life.

Claire scrunched her nose. Could Libby figure it out? Without Claire's help?

Father, give me wisdom. I love her so much. Will You lead her down the right path? I want her to be happy.

Claire's phone rang, and her eyes flashed open.

Dad.

"So, what's this about your sister calling off the wedding?" He sounded exasperated. She could relate.

"Yeah, she peeled out of Aunt Sally's a little while ago."

"Did Sally talk some sense into her?"

"No, she was getting groceries."

"What is going on in that girl's head? She's not going to find a better guy than Jake. She's making a mistake."

Claire normally would take his approval of Jake as the green light to have a nice, long heart-to-heart with her sister, but she couldn't. Not this time. "She's twenty-one, Dad. She can make her own decisions. We'll have to be extra supportive and pray she'll come around."

A long silence stretched.

"Dad? Are you still there?"

"I'm here. I get what you're saying, but I don't like it. What if she doesn't come around?"

"Then it will be for the best." How Claire longed to trust the words she'd uttered. What if she was wrong? And it turned Libby into a miserable man hater?

They said goodbye, and she hung up. She could use a sounding board. Or a distraction. A pontoon ride. A kiss...

But Reed wasn't a distraction. The way she'd started thinking about him nonstop—even more than she thought about working at the zoo—made him the opposite of a distraction. Obsession, more like it. And she shouldn't be doing this...this flirting and hanging out and hoping.

Too familiar. These feelings had been there with Justin, and she'd thrown away too much. Lost too much.

Besides, Reed had his own work to do. Reports and bids and things related to his vice president job. Tasks that didn't involve Lake Endwell. Or her.

Keep me strong, Lord. Keep me focused.

Flaming orange gave way to rich purple as the sun dropped on the horizon the next night. The lake shimmered with reflected colors. Reed never tired of the sight. He sat in a lounge chair on the deck and sipped an ice tea. Sally had brought a pitcher over earlier. This one was pomegranate flavored. One of her best.

He couldn't remember a time he'd been this spoiled.

He'd better not get used to it.

Gulping down another drink, he slid his finger over his phone. Although work hours were long over, John wouldn't mind the interruption for an update. The reports Reed had gone over all afternoon showed profits, growth and all-around success. Too bad the reports were slowly driving him bonkers.

Before arriving in Lake Endwell, he hadn't factored in the differences between being a senior project manager and vice president. His old position involved making calls, meeting with clients, stopping in at job sites and generally moving around. Basically, what he'd been doing here in town. But the vice president's duties seemed to be about one thing: poring over reports.

Maybe he wasn't being fair. Working remotely meant paperwork and phone calls. When Reed took the VP position, he would naturally travel, visit job sites and be more active—wouldn't he?

He sighed. Part of the problem lived next door. He'd missed Claire today. Studying dull statements meant no smiles, no teasing, no car rides around Lake Endwell. No whiffs of coconut lotion.

He dialed John's number.

"Hey, how are you doing, Reed? Out of the cast yet?"

"Not yet. I can't wait to get it off, though."

"I'm sure. So, when are we going to see you around here again?"

Two ducks soared overhead. The gentle laps of the lake against the shore were the only sounds. A vision of busy streets, sirens, horns blaring and all the other things he thought of as home came to mind. "I probably won't be able to drive until a few days before our Denver trip. Once I get back to Chicago, we can fly out there together."

John chuckled. "Glad to hear the fresh air hasn't changed you."

"I'm enjoying it. But I'd have lost it a week ago if I wasn't organizing the crews in town. Looks like we'll have a good shot at preserving the historical feel of this place."

"Good. Good."

Reed hesitated, wanting to be as up-front with his boss as possible. "John, can I ask you something? And I don't want you to be offended."

"Your honesty is why I trust you enough to make you my right-hand man."

"I know, and I appreciate it. But the more I work on these reports, the more I'm wondering how much time I'll be spending at my desk as VP."

"There *is* a lot more paperwork with this position. I'll be the first to admit it. But there's also more travel. Like Denver. And San Diego in August. And we've got other potential clients all fall. You'll be working with me to land the biggest customers, and I know you're the best."

"Thanks, John."

"Take care of your leg."

Reed set his phone on the side table and took another drink of tea. In his quest to secure the VP title, he hadn't put enough thought into the actual position. Nonstop travel, endless reports—neither appealed as much as he'd thought. Maybe the fresh air *was* getting to him.

He replayed John's words, let them soak into his consciousness. *You're the best. I trust you...* Words he'd never heard from anyone else. He'd earned them. Rockbend Construction was the closest thing Reed had to a family, and he wouldn't throw it away.

He glanced at Claire's yellow cottage.

But something more lived next door, wore sparkly tank tops and smelled like the beach.

She'd started bridging the gap between him and Dad. Healing the scars with Dad wouldn't alter Reed's reality. It only made him consider something he'd never let cross his mind.

A relationship.

Lake Endwell.

The people in town appreciated his help and acted like he belonged there. All because of Claire and Dale. The attention was making him forget how easily appreciation and the sense of belonging could disappear.

Maybe he needed to spend less time with his attractive neighbor. How could he get her off his mind if they were together all the time? Every minute in Claire's presence drew him closer to her and farther from the vice president title rightfully his. Her dad had offered time and again to drive anywhere Reed needed to go. He dialed Dale's number.

"Yoo-hoo, Reed, it's me." Claire arrived at Reed's cottage that night.

"Out here, Claire." His voice came from the deck. She slid open the patio door and joined him. Dusk had fallen. She plugged in the strings of patio lights strung through the deck railing. Tiny white sparkles made the space festive. Romantic.

"How did your reports go?" She sat next to him and pretended to study his face. "You look awfully tan. You skipped the boring stuff and sat out here, didn't you?"

"Caught me." He raised his hands, his eyes twinkling.

She laughed. "Did you get everything done?"

"I did. Everything is set for me to fly to Denver with John on July 15."

Her spirits nose-dived at the mention of leaving. "Funny how time flies."

"I can't wait to get out of this cast and in the driver's seat of my truck. I miss my apartment." His firm tone left no argument.

Could she blame him? If their roles were reversed, she'd be homesick too. "Remind me what's in Denver?"

He filled her in on the hospital addition, the work involved, how important it was to clinch the deal. The expressions playing across his face made him look alive, passionate. Obviously, his job filled him with vitality. She asked questions sporadically and took note of his answers. His life in Chicago sounded exciting. Nothing like life here.

She fought to keep her smile in place. As much as she enjoyed listening to him, her insides churned at the truth. She might belong in Lake Endwell, but Reed belonged in Chicago. And all this time driving around town with him had eroded her dedication to getting the zoo job. She'd barely prepared for her interview, and it was set for tomorrow.

"Oh, you don't have to pick me up tomorrow afternoon," Reed said. "Your dad is going to drive me to meet with the new project manager in charge of the buildings downtown. Did Dale ever work in construction?"

Her mind reeled. He wanted Dad to drive him? Not her? Why was she so disappointed? She shook her head. "Construction? Not that I know of."

"Hmm. He knows a lot. Seems to enjoy it."

"Yeah." Her voice sounded weak. She infused iron into it. He'd given her an excuse to refocus on her priority— the zoo job. If she protected her heart in the process, so be it. "That works out better for me. My interview with Tina is tomorrow."

"That's right." His gaze seemed to see right through her. "Everything will work out the way you hoped."

Everything? She peeked at his face. Not quite. But no one got *everything* they wanted. She girded her shoulders. "Will you be okay on your own for dinner tomorrow night?"

"I'm watching the game at Tommy and Bryan's." He avoided eye contact with her.

"Oh." She plastered a smile on and stood. Replaced by her Dad and brothers. Great. "Okay. Well, I'd better get back. See you…sometime."

Marching down the ramp with her back straight, she tried not to let her emotions give her away. Because if Claire knew anything at all, she knew what had just happened.

She'd been dismissed.

As usual.

Chapter Eleven

"Yes, they're wonderful. Look at how they've grown." Claire smiled as Hansel chased Gretel around the backyard Wednesday afternoon. Tina had insisted on conducting the interview here to see the otters for herself. Claire held up a finger. "Give me a minute and I'll get you their growth charts."

"These two do look lively." Standing on the deck, Tina watched the otters interact. The tall, solid woman reminded Claire of a gym coach. She wore her light brown hair short without the aid of hair products. Her burgundy shirt, knee-length khaki shorts, white gym socks and matching orthopedic shoes gave her a no-nonsense air.

Claire flitted to her home office, found the files and hurried back.

"You're doing a good job," Tina said, scanning the sheets. "Surpassing my expectations."

Her chest tightened. It felt good to be praised. "Thank you. It means a lot to me. Hansel and Gretel are a pleasure to care for. They're easy to love."

"I never expected the temporary arrangement would last this long."

"It's no problem. My yard suits them fine. They'll enjoy

their state-of-the-art facilities soon. The quarantine will only be thirty days, right?"

"Yes. Is the feeding arrangement still working for you?"

"They can't get enough of the fish. Little gluttons."

Tina nodded, a serious expression on her sturdy face. "Will you be willing to help get them acclimated?"

Claire's breath caught. Tina had given her an opportunity to negotiate for the job. Should she? Or was it manipulative? *Lord, show me the way.*

"Of course I'll help get them settled. Ideally, I want to check on them every day. That's one of the reasons I applied for the full-time position."

Tina assessed her. Then she rested her thick forearms on the deck rail. "You really want the job, don't you?"

"I do."

"When you filled out your application for Louise's position, I was surprised."

Claire frowned. Why would Tina be surprised? Had she heard the lies Mark spread?

Tina continued. "Your current job has regular hours and is—what—a mile away? You'd be trading it for a thirty-to-forty-minute commute and a hectic schedule working weekends. I'm sure I don't need to tell you about our budget concerns either. We never know when we'll have to make cuts. Are you sure you want it?"

"I'm no longer working for Tammy's clinic, but even if I was, I would want the position." Claire held her head high. "Every job has its rewards, but my heart lives at the zoo. To be given the chance to work with the same animals every day? It's the opportunity of a lifetime for me."

A pleased gleam lit Tina's eye. "Louise still has two weeks left. We'll be making our decision before she leaves. Your dedication has been noted, not only by me, but by most of the staff."

Claire nodded, unsure how to respond.

"Thanks for letting me come over." Tina pushed away from the handrail.

"Anytime."

She walked Tina to her car, waved as she drove away and skipped back inside. Tina might come across as stern, but she had a good, sincere heart.

Claire grabbed her phone, ready to call Reed and share the meeting, but she stopped. By working with Dad and spending nights with her brothers, he'd made it clear he wasn't as into her as she'd hoped.

The gentle pullback. The move that said "if I make other plans, eventually she'll get the hint I'm not interested anymore." She'd been subject to it before. It forced her to be less needy. To lower her expectations. Be less demanding.

And where had it gotten her?

Spinning in a slow circle, she took in her house, the view of the lake, the deck off the dining room.

It had gotten her here, and here was a good place to be.

She had no reason to complain. She had enough. Those other guys wouldn't have made her happy. In fact, she could be like her brothers, with a stack of divorce papers in her office and pockets full of regrets. If Reed was cooling off, so be it.

She was nobody's Tuesday girl.

She'd be an every-day, every-hour, every-second girl, or none at all.

Somehow Reed hadn't realized how much he'd miss Claire. Dinners didn't taste as good. And as much as Reed enjoyed hanging out with her brothers, he missed Claire's shining eyes, her opinions on movies, her insights about life.

He missed Claire.

"My buddy's wife works for Channel 8, and she said the festival next year will be widely covered. Their station loves feel-good stories. All the area papers will help spread the word. City council ran into a few snags on funding. Seems there's an it's-not-fair cry being yelled by the unaffected businesses. They want upgrades sponsored by the town too. Kind of see their point, but…not really. Selfish, you know? Hey, did you find out if those construction firms will offer a discount in exchange for free advertising?"

Reed's head spun with all the information Dale spewed, but Reed liked a man who got things done. And Dale definitely got things done.

"Two are considering it." Reed waited for Dale to park before carefully stepping out and pulling his crutches from the truck bed. "Three won't budge on price."

"Let's hope they come around. Fund-raising will get us far, but not the whole way." Dale hustled to the front sidewalk and opened the door to Uncle Joe's Restaurant. "Let's see how the kitchen's shaping up."

Reed followed him into the dining hall and inhaled the faint aroma of deep-fried everything. He stood in the exact spot he'd been when he picked up Claire the night of the tornado. Longing punched him in the gut—longing to text her, call her, find out what she'd been doing.

This spend-less-time-with-her idea wasn't getting her off his mind. In fact, it only seemed to be drawing her closer to the zoo.

Claire was the one who blew him off today. Said she had business with the otters. What kind of business did a person have with an otter?

Reed made his way to the doorway of the kitchen and paused.

"The new ten-burner gas range will be in next week. No, not there. The deep fryers go in the corner." Sally's voice grew louder from the kitchen until she appeared in the dining room. "Reed! What a nice surprise. Where's Claire?"

"Not sure." Time to change the subject. "Did you see the Johnsons' roof? Looks pretty good. The tarp's gone."

Frowning, she wiped her hands together. "Well, that's terrific about the roof, but why isn't Claire with you? She didn't say a word to me about having other plans."

How was he supposed to answer? *She prefers otters to me…*

Sally's eyebrows drew together. "Libby's canceling the wedding must have knocked some of her brains loose. Claire's always dropped everything at the hint of a crisis with one of her brothers or Libby. She's got to learn to put herself first sometimes. Libby isn't going to fall apart if Claire helps you."

The wedding was off? Reed's mind spun. Why hadn't Jake called him?

A knot of uneasiness built in his chest. A better question would be why Reed hadn't called Jake all week. And now Sally thought Claire was to blame for not being with him, when it wasn't the entire truth.

"Actually, Sally, I asked Dale to drive with me a few days this week."

"I'd better get over there." Sally searched through her purse, pulled out her keys and walked toward the door, muttering, "Might not get the zoo job she's been obsessed with for years. Plus, Libby's a wreck, which makes her a wreck. Now this." The door closed behind her.

Acid rose in his stomach. Put like that…

Claire wasn't making him handle the town stuff on her own. If he had to guess, he'd say she was avoiding him.

Did he blame her? He'd asked her dad to drive him around and flat out told her he was out of there mid-July.

He was a jerk. Selfish. He wouldn't be surprised if she

put him in the same category as the old boyfriend she told him about.

Dale strode into the dining room. "All set here, Reed. How about I take you out for pizza?"

"I'll have to pass this time." He had some making up to do. Starting with Jake. "Would you mind dropping me off at Jake's apartment?"

"Not at all. Have you there in a jiffy."

They drove through terrain familiar to Reed. The DeMarcos' house—roof repaired last week. Claire had taken plenty of before and after pictures. He could still see her sparkling eyes as she snapped the photos. Miss Gert's place—new sunroom to confine Whiskers. Reed's gut clenched at the sight of fresh lumber stacked outside JoJo's Jewelry. He and Claire had personally spent an hour with JoJo's husband, now in his eighties, discussing what was best for the store, even though JoJo had died years ago and their daughter now ran the shop. That was what Reed liked about Claire—she cared. She cared about the people who had started it all.

Reed glanced at Dale. Window rolled down. Late sun hitting the dash. Contentment filled his weathered face.

Lake Endwell would get along fine without Reed Hamilton. Just fine. So why did he have a sinking sensation in his soul?

Dale parked in front of Jake's apartment. "Call if you need a ride home, son."

Son. The sinking sensation deepened. "Thanks. I will."

Dale drove away, and Reed called Jake on his cell phone. "Hey, can you meet me out front so I don't have to walk up the steps with my crutches?"

Jake loped down the steps, looking as if he hadn't slept in days.

"Hey, man." Jake rubbed his hands over his stubble. "What brings you here?"

"Haven't seen you in a while."

"Yeah, well…"

In person, Jake's sadness seemed more real, as if Reed could reach out and touch it. Life was easier to handle when he was in Chicago. A couple calls a month and his duty was done. But this? What could he say?

"Is there anywhere outside we could sit?" Reed craned his neck to find a common area.

Jake let out a pitiful sigh. "Over here." They walked past a row of apartments to a small courtyard with benches and flowers. "I guess you heard."

"Yeah." Reed nodded.

"I miss her."

"I know."

"Every time I think about her, I wonder what went wrong. I tried to get our wedding pushed up as soon as possible, but everything I did made her mad."

"None of this was your fault."

"Easy for you to say. You're not in love with the most infuriating and beautiful female in the county."

How to respond to that line of reasoning?

"I don't want to talk about her anyhow."

Good. Reed didn't know what to say, so not talking about Libby made that easier.

Jake gestured to his cast. "How's your leg? Ready to get back to work?"

"Yeah. I'm going back soon."

"Don't sound so enthusiastic." The hint of a smile crossed Jake's lips.

"I'm nervous. Not about being vice president, but there's a lot more paperwork than I expected."

"You seem to like organizing the buildings around town." Jake thought a moment. "Why don't you do it full-time?"

"You mean quit my job?" He'd never—not once—

considered quitting the place he felt most at home. He'd spent close to a decade building his reputation at Rock-bend Construction. He couldn't—wouldn't—up and leave it. "No."

"You have enough skills to work in commercial or residential real estate. And you'd be coming to Michigan at a good time. A lot of the builders moved out of state when the recession hit. With the housing market picking up, there's less competition. Higher demand."

"You seem to know a lot about this." Reed tried on the idea, but it didn't make sense, not when he had an incredible job waiting in Chicago. "I don't want to work for a home builder. It would be too big a step down."

"Who said anything about working for one?" Jake leveled a "don't be an idiot" look his way. "You have all you need to start your own company."

His own company.

Reed had dreamed about it off and on over the years, but he also fantasized about running a marathon or spending a year in Europe. He had never run more than two miles, and he couldn't see himself taking a year off for anything. The month in Alaska was the closest he'd ever come to a real vacation.

"You could live in Lake Endwell. With the city nearby and all the small towns, you'd stay busy."

"Hold on." Reed stretched his arm out. "I'm not starting a business in Lake Endwell."

"Why not?"

"Town's too small. I wouldn't have enough work."

"Didn't you hear a word I said? You'd have plenty of work. You could target the whole county. Building, remodeling, restoration—you name it."

"I can't." Reed curled his hands into fists.

"Can't or won't?" Jake sounded mad. "Guess all my

suggestions are stupid. Libby thinks so. You obviously do too."

"Hold on. I never said the idea was stupid. And you're the smartest guy I know. I wouldn't have lasted one semester in the engineering department, and you're working for General Motors now."

How could he explain to Jake that Lake Endwell was too difficult for him? He already liked Claire and her family a little too much. That the overwhelming Sheffield embrace drew him in, made him want to be part of it, part of a family—part of their family.

Reed couldn't take losing them too.

"Come on, Jake. Let's order a pizza and watch the game."

"Maybe another time." Dejection filled his tone. "I'll take you home."

Great. Now he'd upset Jake. This was why he kept a distance and didn't make an effort. He wasn't any good at it.

The next morning, Reed drew a deep breath, clutched the stems of wildflowers in his hand and tottered on one crutch as he knocked on Claire's door. He might not be good at making an effort, but he had to try. Claire deserved it.

He wiped his free hand down his shirt. Why was he so nervous? He wasn't a stranger to being around women. He'd brought girls flowers on occasion. In the past he'd been sure of himself, confident. But now? He wouldn't be surprised if his voice cracked and sweat beaded on his forehead when she opened the door.

If she opened the door.

Maybe he should forget about this and go fishing for a while. Save them both the heartache.

The door flung open, and there she was. Claire. Beautiful, kind, biggest-smile-he'd-ever-seen Claire.

Her eyes lit like the Ferris wheel on Navy Pier. But they dimmed as quickly. She took a step back. "What are you doing here? Shouldn't you be out with Dad?"

He thrust the flowers to her. "I heard the forecast say a tornado might be coming through. I figured we could weather it out together. For old times' sake."

The momentary uncertainty he'd glimpsed dissolved when she laughed—the laugh he'd come to anticipate.

"Get in here." She waved him inside, lifting the bouquet to her nose and inhaling. "These are gorgeous. They smell good too. Thank you."

"So, the otters? How did your thing go?"

"Good. Remember how I told you my friend Lisa owns the animal sanctuary? I went over there to see how Hansel and Gretel's mother is doing. She's getting around much better. And my interview with Tina went well. I think I have a good shot at the job."

"That's great." He took in her living room again, surprised at how much it felt like home. "How are the wild animals anyway?"

"I'm assuming you mean my dear, sweet otter babies. They're getting big," she called over her shoulder on her way to the kitchen. He followed her. She opened a cupboard and found a crystal vase. "Want to see them?"

He wanted to see her. He couldn't get enough—the graceful line of her arm as she flipped on the faucet. The way her hair fell as she arranged the flowers. The quick lift of her head and flash of a smile telling him how pleased she was he'd stopped by.

He cleared his throat. Equally pleased. "Are they outside?"

He and Claire settled in the lawn chairs and tossed rubber squeak toys to the energetic pair.

"You never answered my question. Off day at the office? And by office, I mean Dad's truck." Claire blinked those hypnotizing eyes at him. A trace of bitterness seeped into her tone.

I had to see you. You make me feel like the man I want to be.

"No. I wanted to see you." He tapped his fingers against his cast.

The corner of her lips tipped up in an awkward smile, one that hinted she understood.

Did she? Did she know how much she meant to him? How terrifying it was?

Reed gripped the arms of the lawn chair. "I'm going to be brutally honest. Your dad wore me out."

Her laugh rang through the air. "Dad is full of energy."

And just like that, they were back to comfortable. Reed shook his head. How did she make it so easy?

He brought his palms together. "If I beg hard enough, will you drive me to the restaurant later? I want to check the industrial outlets."

"Start begging." Her chin tipped up, and playfulness crinkled the corners of her eyes. "A little flattery might help your cause."

He smiled. Flattery? No problem. "I need you, Claire. No one can drive an outdated, rusty four-door car like you. You make the drive smell good, like suntan lotion. Your dad's truck smells like bait. Nightcrawlers, to be specific. And you're prettier than your dad, but don't tell him I said so. By the way, why don't you own a newer vehicle? Seems like you'd get a discount."

She threw a tennis ball at his chest, but he caught it and grinned.

"My car is not rusty. I'm attached to it. And yes, I'll drive you. Not like I have anything else to do. I did research three veterinary clinics in Kalamazoo to apply for if the zoo job falls through, but I'm waiting until I get a definitive answer from Tina. And you need to prepare yourself for the Fourth of July celebration. It will be here this Thursday already."

"Fourth of July," Reed said. "Summer's passing quickly." The otters groomed themselves in the sun. Funny little guys.

"Soon you'll be in your big corner office as the vice president, and, hopefully, I'll be making the commute to the zoo every day."

"Yeah." Leaving Claire in a few weeks had to happen, but the promotion sounded less promising than it had when he arrived in town. Jake's suggestion trickled back, but he shoved it aside to think about later. "Talked to Libby lately? Jake's a mess."

"She's been keeping to herself." She lifted one tanned shoulder. "I hope they work it out. They seem right for each other, you know?"

"Yeah, they do." He hesitated. Now that he was here, he had questions. Questions he shouldn't be thinking, let alone asking. "What about you?"

"What about me?"

"You told me a while back the pickings here were slim. But let's say some great guy appeared. Would you reconsider?"

Reed could kick himself. Why had he asked her that? Now she'd think he was hinting. Which he was. But wasn't. Not marriage. Not him.

"Reconsider what? Dating?" She looked nauseous. "No."

"More than dating. Marriage. Forever. Let's say, an imaginary guy. One who loves animals and puts you first."

"I don't know." She mindlessly brushed dust off the arm of the chair. "Imaginary guys don't exist. I don't think about it much anymore. Did your broken leg get you thinking about forever, or did Jake and Libby have you pondering?"

"Jake and Libby." He grew serious. "I've never let a woman get close enough to share forever."

She flashed him a wide-eyed glance. "Why?"

He shrugged. "Wish I had the answer, Claire." The answer kicked him square in the chest. Fear. Normally, he'd shove that information right back into his subconscious, but not this time. "My mom's death screwed me up."

She studied him. "Are you afraid of dying?"

"Not today." He grinned. "Eventually." He ripped a piece of grass from the ground and twisted it. "The fear isn't about me. I know God has a room prepared for me when my time on earth is over."

"You're afraid of losing another family."

"Anyone I love." He'd never admitted it before. Never put it in words. He'd lost too many people he loved.

Wind rustled the leaves of the oak. Bright yellow and orange marigolds swayed. Peaceful.

"I'm afraid of losing my family too. That's why I don't take living here for granted."

Of course she belonged in Lake Endwell with her family. The town had grown on him too. But what if six months from now things cooled between him and Claire? Her family and the community wouldn't accept him the way they did now. And even if they did, he'd always be on edge. Wondering if he'd drive Claire away the way he had everyone else.

Chapter Twelve

"Are you comfortable?" Claire asked. "We can sit somewhere else if you want."

Sitting next to Reed in the pew Sunday morning brought flurries to Claire's stomach. He smelled clean and masculine, and boy, did that dress shirt and crimson necktie look good on him! She bounced with anticipation at the surprise she had for him after church.

"I'm fine." He squirmed in his seat.

"You are not." She started to rise, but his hand on her arm stopped her.

"We're not moving."

She narrowed her eyes, but Libby's cough from the other side of Dad got her attention. Libby, her face drawn, shot Claire a dirty look and mouthed, "Why is he here?"

Claire almost rolled her eyes. Libby had been more than vocal about how she never wanted to see Jake or anyone in his family again. Too bad. Claire had been praying every night for the Lord to heal Libby's heart. And though Claire constantly wrestled with wanting to swoop in and fix all of Libby's problems, she'd refrained.

Spending the past two days with Reed had helped. After their talk Friday, she drove him to the restaurant, then to job sites to check on their progress. Four of the five building owners approved the blueprints, while one wanted to add an apartment above for rental purposes. The new foundations were scheduled for Monday.

As the pastor opened the service with a prayer, Claire added one of her own. *Thank You for sending Reed to town. He breathed new life into this place.*

Reed's deep voice joined the other congregants for the first verse of the hymn. As he began to sing "All Glory, Laud, and Honor," her heart throbbed, expanded. She added another prayer.

How did You know, God? How did You know I needed him? Reed's important to me, one of my best friends. I know he can't stay. But what will I do without him?

Her heart whispered to pray for a way to be with Reed. She could not consider moving away from her family again. And not for a guy, even if the guy was Reed. Not when her dream job finally opened up. The whole thing was like a terrible case of déjà vu.

And what if she started praying, only to end up in Chicago? What if she didn't mean as much to Reed as he did to her? She'd be a Tuesday girl. Again. God wouldn't be that cruel. He wouldn't ask her to give it all up.

Would He?

Her hands grew clammy. She folded them together, gripping until the knuckles turned white. No point in thinking about it today. She still had time with Reed. Maybe her feelings would change. The attraction would fade.

And in the meantime, she'd enjoy Reed for what he was—a good friend.

One she'd kissed. One she wanted to see every morning, afternoon and night.

The service sped by, and soon they made their way onto the lush grass of the front lawn.

"Reed, just the man I wanted to see." Leroy Oakhurst, a congregant who Reed and Claire had contacted after the tornado, strode to them. "Can't thank you enough for all you did for my uncle. His farm's been here for over a hundred years. Now that the barn's scheduled to be rebuilt, he acts twenty years younger."

Reed's neck grew red, but he shook Leroy's meaty hand. "Glad to help. Your uncle told me he'd wanted to replace the barn for some time. At least some good came out of this, right?"

Leroy chuckled. "You can say that again. If I had known getting the barn up meant so much to him, I would have helped him long ago."

After Leroy left, Claire placed her hand on Reed's biceps. Still muscle-y. "I have a surprise."

He leaned in close enough for her to feel his breath on her cheek. "What kind of surprise?"

She gulped. "The fund-raising sign is ready. Want to help me pound it in place?"

"Of course." He followed her to her car. "Do I get to see it first?"

She buckled herself in and grinned. "Nope. You have to wait until we install it."

"What if I turn around and sneak a peek? What are you going to do?"

"Don't you dare!"

He laughed. Seconds later, she pulled in front of the white gazebo at City Park. She dragged the large wooden sign covered with a sheet from her backseat. "I'm popping the trunk. Grab the hammer and mallet for me, will you?"

"Yes, boss." Reed disappeared behind her car.

She heaved the sign to the spot the park director and garden club had approved. Reed thunked behind her with the tools.

"Want me to do this?" he asked.

"You're on crutches. I had Tommy stop by yesterday to

get a hole started. All we have to do is get the post in, give the sign a few whacks and we'll be good." With Reed's help, Claire maneuvered the sign into the hole, thumped the top with the mallet until it stuck in place and stepped back. "Want to unveil it?"

"I don't know." His eyes shimmered. "You did all the work."

"Go ahead." She grinned, waving the mallet toward him.

He ripped the sheet off and read the sign out loud. "Help rebuild Lake Endwell. Celebrate the restoration on Memorial Weekend!" A drawing of a thermometer with black lines leading up to one hundred thousand dollars filled the sign. The first ten thousand was already filled in red. "How did you raise ten grand already?"

She shrugged. "Dad. He's passionate."

"And generous."

"Well, the town means a lot to us."

Reed took her hand in his. Her heartbeat pounded. "It means a lot to me too."

She wanted to lean in, to kiss him, but she covered his hand with her other one and stepped back. *A good friend.* "Thanks for everything, Reed."

The intensity in his eyes was not helping her racing pulse.

She pulled her hand free. "What do you have planned for this afternoon? We could watch a movie or something."

"I can't," he said, his voice raspy. "I promised John I'd review the hospital bid."

"Okay."

But it wasn't okay. It wasn't okay that one minute she tried to convince herself he was a good friend, and the next she wanted more. Needed more.

This relationship would end.

With Reed hours away and her here. Alone.

* * *

Why had Claire caved in to Aunt Sally's demands for a shopping trip? On a Sunday, no less?

After Claire dropped Reed off at the cottage, Libby came over, and they'd been happy watching *You've Got Mail* and eating their body weight in nachos and ice cream. But no, Aunt Sally forced them from the couch to the mall.

"Three more weeks! The restaurant will be open." Aunt Sally rubbed her hands together so rapidly she could start a fire right there in Macy's women's department. Claire scanned the wall for a fire extinguisher.

"Really?" Claire asked. "I didn't realize the restaurant would be done so soon."

"Reed's been keeping on the contractors and they are flying! Flying, I tell you. I think we'd still be staring at the same pile of rubble if he hadn't stepped in when he did." Sally clutched her purse to her chest. "We'll finally be ready for Friday fish fry again."

Claire's pulse tripped at the mention of Reed, but she doused it with another round of admonitions. He was reviewing the hospital bid right now. The project he would be lining up as vice president. In Chicago. And she should be purchasing sandals or something. Anything to get her mind off him.

"I'm happy for you and Uncle Joe." Libby seized a hot-pink scoop-necked shirt from the rack. "The town isn't the same without the restaurant. I'm ready to sip lemonade from the outdoor patio and listen to Jimmy Buffett."

"We all can't wait to get our hands around one of your bacon cheeseburgers." Claire poked through the shorts, but none caught her eye.

"Too bad Reed will be back in Chicago soon. He fits right in here. But that job of his sure sounds impressive." Aunt Sally held up a white blouse, then hung it back on the rack. Her lashes, thick with mascara, reached for her eyebrows. "Later this summer, girls, we should plan a road trip. I've always wanted to see Shedd Aquarium, Miracle Mile, Navy Pier. Eat Chicago pizza…"

Libby lowered her chin and stabbed Aunt Sally with a lethal glare. "Um, that's in Chicago, Aunt Sally."

"I know."

Libby hitched her chin to Claire. "By the way, thanks a lot for bringing Jake's brother to church. Where is your loyalty? You know how I feel right now."

"We're not in second grade, Libs. Reed's become a good friend. And he hasn't had the easiest of times." It still bothered her he hadn't spent much time with his dad. The ice cream outing had loosened them up, but they needed more time together if they were ever going to work through their issues.

"Well, I haven't either," Libby said. "First the tornado, and then we couldn't reschedule the wedding and now my former fiancé hates me. I wish you'd be more supportive."

A fifty-pound weight landed in Claire's gut. "I *am* supportive. I love you, and it's eating me up that you're miserable. I want nothing more than for you and Jake to get back together."

"We aren't getting back together, and I'd appreciate it if you thought about my feelings once in a while. When I look at Reed, I see all the things about Jake I miss."

Sally snapped her gum. "Maybe that's a good thing, toots."

Claire suppressed a smile at Aunt Sally's fearlessness. "Have you talked to Jake at all?"

"No." Libby's chin rose as her lower lip wobbled. "I called him yesterday and left a message. He didn't call back. It's obvious he's moved on. I must not be very important to him."

Moved on? Based on one unreturned message? Claire

focused on a summery dress in cornflower blue. Short sleeves, full skirt, not too long.

A twinge of jealousy pierced her. All she had with Reed was one kiss and a shared desire to rebuild the town. Not the same as what Libby had with Jake. Not by miles.

"I've been replaying the last months over and over in my mind—" Libby pointed to her head "—it's like a DVD on autoplay up there. You know the truck Jake bought in March? Didn't even discuss it with me. Our honeymoon? Slapped the plans together—honestly, I wouldn't have minded Maine—it just hurt he didn't bother to find out my opinion. And then his relentless pushing to get married on Labor Day…ugh."

"I didn't know that." A dull ache spread over Claire's chest. Why had she put most of the blame on Libby for the breakup? Shouldn't sisters give each other the benefit of the doubt?

"I…" Libby's throat worked. "I tried to overcompensate by demanding what I wanted, but now he thinks I'm a spoiled brat. Maybe I am. I'm not the right girl for him."

"Sounds to me like you need to clear things up," Aunt Sally said. "Go over and talk to the boy."

"I can't, Aunt Sally." Libby slung four shirts over her arm.

"Do you love him?" Sally rested her hand on a display.

"Yes," Libby said.

"Did he beat you?"

Libby pursed her lips. "Come on, you know Jake better than that. He would never lay a hand on me."

"Did you catch him cheating?"

Now Libby looked dumbfounded. "No! He would never cheat on me."

"He swore at you." Sally lifted her index finger. "Got rip-roaring drunk, didn't he?"

"No and no."

"Doesn't want kids? Already has a wife? Doesn't believe in God anymore?"

"Stop." Libby straightened her free arm with her palm out. The hangers dangling from her other arm jingled. "You know none of that is true."

Aunt Sally raised herself to her full height. "Then get the wedding back on. Apologize. Talk like adults."

Claire didn't try to hide her fascination with the scene playing out before her. She'd always admired Aunt Sally, but the woman had risen to heroic proportions just now.

Libby wilted, and she switched the hangers to her other arm. "I don't think I can."

"You're one of the gutsiest girls I know, Libby Sheffield. You have it in you to get Jake back." Aunt Sally folded her arms over her chest.

"What if I make him miserable?" Her watery eyes widened. "What if marrying him makes me miserable?"

Aunt Sally took a step toward Libby. "Honey, you're already miserable. I think you're making a mistake. Marry the boy. He loves you. We all know it. He's not always going to do things your way—no man does. And if you found one who would, well, he wouldn't make you happy. Jake's your equal. Let him be the man you need him to be, and everything else will fall into place."

Claire held her breath, trying to memorize the words, stunned by her aunt's perception. The shirts slipped from Libby's hands to the floor.

"I know you're hurting and confused, Libby, but think about it." Aunt Sally drew Libby to her and they held each other a minute.

Claire waited until they stepped apart, and she put her arm around Aunt Sally's shoulder. "What would we do without you?"

Sally's eyes grew misty. "Aw, I love you girls. You're

like my own. I always wanted a girl, although I love my boys too. I'm glad you never mind me shopping with you."

Libby sniffled, her face blotchy. "You're our favorite shopping partner, right, Claire?"

"Absolutely."

"Look at us, a bunch of teary sad sacks." Sally sniffled, then patted Libby's cheek. "The only time we cry in a store is during bathing suit season, and we already did that last month."

Libby bent to pick up the hangers and shirts. "I'm going to try these on."

"Retail therapy," Sally said. "Works every time."

As Libby headed to the dressing rooms, Aunt Sally turned to Claire. "So, what do you say about that road trip?"

Claire pretended to be enamored with a display of socks. Long socks. Ankle socks. Striped…

"Well?" Aunt Sally drew the word out.

Claire groaned and raised her eyes to the ceiling. "Maybe next year."

"Next year?" she asked. "How about soon? Before fall."

"He hasn't even left." Claire shrugged. "He'll want to get back to his life."

"Have you ever thought about fitting into his life?"

Claire squirmed. It was great when Aunt Sally leveled Libby with the truth, but having her intuition skewer her? "I don't see that happening."

"Just because you took a chance once and it didn't work out the way you planned doesn't mean you have to live here forever. If you love him, you can make it work. Now I'm going to the petite section. The apple-green top over there is calling my name."

Love him? *Love?* Aunt Sally must have started watching the afternoon soap operas again. Claire didn't love Reed. She *liked* him. Enjoyed their conversations. Thought he was attractive in a "get the heart paddles, women are collapsing" sort of way. Might be tempted to kiss him again.

Stop thinking about him!

She pushed a sweatshirt out of the way.

And not live in Lake Endwell? That was crazy talk. Claire wasn't leaving. Couldn't leave. Who would be there for Libby? Her brothers? The otters? They were her life. She wasn't moving away from them. Not for anything.

Especially not for the flightiest thing of all.

Love.

Chapter Thirteen

Reed slowly progressed to the dock, where the entire Sheffield clan busied themselves erecting a white tent and setting up tables, chairs and coolers. The pristine green lawn surrounded by shrubs and flowers—big purple and blue hydrangeas, Sally called them—could have been a photograph in a magazine. Yesterday morning while he and Dale checked on the restaurant's tile installation, Claire had planted red, white and blue pinwheels all around his yard.

Well, it wasn't *his* yard—just his for another week or so. But the infamous Fourth of July party had arrived, which meant he had to share Claire today. With her family. Half the town.

But not Jake.

At church on Sunday, Libby had made it clear she resented any Hamilton presence in her vicinity. Reed's skin had practically burned from the scorching glares she'd sent him. He doubted Jake would be invited to the festivities. Reed hadn't had the heart to ask him about it, though.

Last night, at Reed's request, Jake had stopped by. The short sentences Reed got out of him weren't much better than the sorrowful sag of his face. Jake had to snap out of it, and soon.

Maybe he should support his brother and skip the Sheffield shindig. Go over to Jake's instead.

But he'd miss Claire.

At some point, he'd have to get used to the sensation.

Problem was, he didn't want to. In fact, everything inside him wanted to stay. To flirt. To see her smile, eat barbecue next to her, sneak a kiss under the fireworks.

"What do you think of the tile we picked out, Reed?" Sally bustled to him, wiping her hands on the back of her tight denim shorts. She wore long star-shaped earrings that sparkled as she moved. Naturally, she gave him a hug.

"Looks great." He tried not to sneeze at her overpowering floral body spray. "You'll have no trouble meeting your reopening date. You throwing a party for it?"

She looked at him as if he'd grown an extra arm. "What kind of question is that? Of course we're throwing a party! And we expect you to be there. Two weeks from Saturday."

"I might be in Denver."

"You can make it back. We'll dish up the best fish fry you ever tasted." She scanned the yard. "Oh, Claire, Claire! Look who's here. Reed!"

"It's not a surprise, Aunt Sally. He *is* staying at the cottage." Claire approached, her arms laden with bags of plastic silverware and napkins. He tried not to stare but couldn't help himself.

"I know," Sally said. "But he's on those doggone crutches and needs someone to keep him company. Come over here."

"I am over here."

"Well…" For once, Sally was at a loss for words. "I'd better check on the food. Is Jake coming? I called him earlier and told him he'd better get his buns to the cottage or I would drag him myself."

Reed blinked and then frowned. Had Libby and Jake

gotten back together in the wee hours of the morning or something?

"If Libby isn't the right girl for him, fine," Sally continued. "But he needs to get out. Celebrating our nation's independence will be good for him."

Claire nodded. "I agree."

Reed's mouth dropped open as he glanced at Sally, then Claire, then back at Sally. They meant it. They wanted Jake there. Whether he and Libby were a couple or not.

The concept didn't add up. Like a broken circuit or a doorway without steps leading to it, he couldn't make sense of it.

He'd been sure Jake would be shunned. It was how the world worked.

Or maybe…

Maybe it was just how *his* world worked.

"Come on." Claire transferred the silverware into Sally's hands, grabbed Reed's shirt and tugged. "You can help me put the potato salad in bowls."

He set the crutches in motion to follow her up the ramp to the upper deck and inside. The kitchen remained empty except for the counter full of potato chips, buns, pickle jars and packages of sparklers.

"I'm happy you're here to celebrate this with us, Reed."

He couldn't stop the ticker tape of questions rolling through. Such as, why was she happy? They'd spent their usual time making calls and driving to job sites each afternoon, but she'd made plans Monday night with Libby, and he'd gone to her brothers' house on Tuesday.

Would she still be happy when he left? Was he like a spare family member—similar to an adopted distant cousin—to be included in the picnic? Or was he more?

He wanted to be more.

His gaze skimmed her shiny, dark hair. The smattering of freckles the sun had coaxed to her nose. Her slim legs peeking out from underneath her shorts. The white tank top with glittery pink lettering that spelled out Peace, Love and Hipponess.

Which reminded him…

"Wait right here. I have something for you." He clopped to the bedroom and rummaged through his closet until he found the box FedEx had delivered yesterday. He returned to the kitchen.

"What's this?" She accepted the package with a questioning glance.

"Open it and see." He grinned. She was going to love it. It was all Claire.

She slid out the heather-gray T-shirt, unfolded it and laughed. "Otterly Adorable?"

"I saw it and couldn't resist."

Grinning, she held it to her chest, and he gave her a thumbs-up.

"Perfect," she said. "Or wait, 'Otterly Adorable.' I love it!" She closed the distance between them, wriggled her arms over his shoulders and hugged him. He inhaled coconuts and held her tightly.

He didn't want to let her go.

Ever.

Her face tipped up and he lost all thoughts except how much he wanted to kiss her. How those exotic eyes hypnotized him. How Claire Sheffield had come to dominate his thoughts. Day and night.

He lowered his head, ready to capture her lips…

"Oh! Sorry. Didn't mean to interrupt."

Claire lurched back, a blush rising to her cheeks. "You weren't interrupting, Aunt Sally. Reed was just…um…look at my cute shirt." She held the shirt up, and Sally grinned, nodding at supersonic speed.

"Ooh, nice, it's you. Now, let me get the matches and I'll be out of here. Then you two can go back to…whatever you were doing." She gave them a sly look, whisked the box of matches from the drawer and sauntered back outside.

"Oh, my word. That was so embarrassing." Claire slumped, resting her hand against the counter.

"Kind of like getting caught by Mom."

"Exactly." She giggled, lifting her hand to her mouth. "You and I never had the chance to get caught by our moms, though, did we?"

Her humor ignited his, and he chuckled. "No. I guess that's one good thing, right?"

She grew more serious. "Aunt Sally stepped into the role for Libby and me. We're pretty blessed."

He touched her hair, letting it slide through his fingers. "It's funny, but Sally kind of stepped into the role for me since I've been here. She's something."

"She is," Claire said.

The sliding door opened, and Libby stalked inside. "There you are." She popped a hand on each hip as lasers blasted from her tired eyes. "Who invited Jake?"

Reed straightened. *Here it comes.*

Claire withered at Libby's interruption. Just when she'd gotten Reed alone and almost kissed him, and he revealed more of his feelings—even if they were about Aunt Sally— Libby had to go and ruin the moment.

Claire lifted her chin. "I invited him. Dad invited him. Aunt Sally invited him. We *all* invited him."

"Who gave you the right?"

She stepped forward. "You did."

"I did?" Libby let out a brittle laugh. "I did not."

"You did the minute you accepted his proposal."

"Which I unaccepted, but no one here seems to have gotten the memo."

Claire leveled a titanium-hard stare at Libby. "Jake lives here. I'm not cutting him off."

"But you'll cut me off. Great, Claire. You prefer him to me."

"I don't. I love you. But I'm not going to treat Jake differently now. It's not right, and you know it."

"Says who?" Libby asked.

"Says the Bible."

Libby's face grew ruddy as she pressed her lips together. Her expression morphed from angry to uncertain and finally to sad. Claire held her breath, her soul cracking at hurting her feelings. This week had been awful for Libby—but Claire wouldn't shun Jake. She couldn't. It was wrong.

Libby hung her head. "You're right."

Had she heard Libby correctly? Claire exhaled. Leaning against the counter, Reed shrugged as if to say he was surprised too.

"Do you want to talk, Libs?" Claire gestured to the empty deck. "We can go outside."

"No. I...I've got to find...Dad." Libby, teary-eyed, practically ran outside.

Reed set his hand on Claire's shoulder. "You amaze me."

"Why? Because I hurt my sister's feelings? I'm so tired of wondering what to do. I keep trying to help her, but I end up hurting her."

He cupped her chin. "You did help her. And Jake. Not many people would welcome him in this situation."

His words repaired the pocket of guilt she'd grown weary of trying to keep shut. "Everyone would welcome Jake. He's a great guy. We love him."

"You know what I mean."

She nodded.

They stood there, touching, close, silent. The steady hum of cars arriving shook her out of their connection.

"Looks like it's party time." Reed peered out the window.

"We'd better get this potato salad ready or we're going

to be in trouble." Claire searched for large plastic serving bowls. "Grab the big spoons. They're in the drawer next to the stove."

They spent the next twenty minutes transferring food to bowls, opening chips and covering everything with an abundance of plastic wrap that refused to stay put.

"Who invented this stuff?" Reed wrestled a long rectangle of wrap determined to crinkle into itself. "They should be thrown in jail."

"It's the worst. I'll see if there's some foil we can use instead." She sifted through the drawer.

Heavy footsteps alerted her to her brothers' arrival. They greeted Reed, then surrounded the island like a pack of wolves circling a downed deer. She shooed them away. "Get out of here. No sneaking food. We won't have any left with you guys around. If you want to help, take those bowls to the tent. Aunt Sally will tell you where to put them."

Bryan and Sam sneaked handfuls of chips. She shifted her weight and gave them long, penetrating stares until they sheepishly obeyed.

"Come on. We're done in here. Let's go eat." She led the way outside, waiting for Reed to clear the door with his crutches, and they joined the growing crowd on the lawn. Claire introduced him to newcomers who arrived.

"Reed Hamilton? *The* Reed Hamilton? Oh, my!" Sandra Dixon, a pleasant middle-aged woman from church, stood in front of Reed. "We've wanted to thank you. You helped get our pole barn scheduled. They're already framing it. Thank you very much." A couple from town flanked Reed, complimenting him and thanking him. Another family joined.

Claire seized the opportunity to slip away. Where was Libby? Claire scanned the yard. Her sister stood next to Jake near the dock. Neither seemed to be speaking, but Jake took Libby's hand, and she didn't yank it away. They strolled away from the party to the lane ribboning around the lake. Maybe they would work it out.

The party continued. Claire and Reed faced mounds of food under the tent while Tommy, Bryan and Sam kept the conversation lively. Claire sneaked smiles their way often. This fun attitude was what she loved most about her brothers. They knew how to make anyone feel like old friends.

Later, someone turned on a country playlist over the speakers. Near the corner, Dad and Uncle Joe guffawed at something. Aunt Sally came over to chat, declaring it the "best Fourth ever," kicked off her star-studded flip-flops and sprawled her legs out on an empty chair.

Libby and Jake reappeared, making their way to the table. Libby's face broke into a magnificent smile. "The wedding's back on!"

Claire hugged them both. "I'm so happy! Congratulations! You two are perfect for each other, and I'm glad you realized it."

Libby twined her arm around Jake's waist, and he hooked his arm over her shoulder as if he never wanted to let her go.

"We're still settling on a date. We're thinking Christmas-ish. I'll be off for school break, and Jake will be able to get time off too." She beamed at Jake.

He didn't tear his gaze from hers. "I told her we could pick any date she wanted—I didn't care—as long as she agreed to spend the rest of her life with me. I can't live without you, Libby."

"I…" Libby said. "Well, this week has been terrible. I don't know how I ever thought I could live without you either."

Jake kissed her, their affection hanging in the air.

"Congratulations." Reed hobbled his way to Jake and hugged him. "I'm happy for you."

"Me too. You know what this means, though?" Jake grinned.

"What?"

"I need you to come back as best man again. Or better yet, stay. Lake Endwell suits you."

Claire held her breath, shocked at the hope Jake's words sent rippling through her.

Reed? Living here?

Could there be a better idea?

Reed's face paled, and he remained silent. Her heart fell—he seemed unenthused about the prospect. In fact, the way he shook his head at Jake gave her the impression they'd discussed the possibility already. Reed clearly did not want to stay in Lake Endwell.

And once again she wondered why she was getting so attached to someone dead set on leaving.

Ready for the fireworks display, Reed sat on the quilt Claire had spread out. The cast still annoyed him. This whole picnic would have been easier to get around if he didn't have crutches. Claire hugged her knees to her chest. Ever since Jake and Libby announced the wedding was back on, she'd been pensive, quiet.

Reed stole another peek at her. He didn't think the wedding was the problem. Maybe it was Jake's untimely crack about Reed living in Lake Endwell. At first, he'd wanted to smack his brother for spilling the idea, certain Libby and Claire would latch on to it. But Claire hadn't. Not at all.

Didn't she want him to stay?

Based on her posture, he'd have to say no.

Jake's idea for him to start his own company had pushed Reed into the category of *considering*, though. Last night, with nothing else to do, he'd researched the competing construction firms, located potential suppliers and listed the subcontractors he'd met during the rebuilding efforts.

That had been more about killing time, though, not going ahead with it.

A breeze cooled his skin as stars flickered on. Claire excused herself, unfolding her legs and climbing the small bank to the lawn. His gut grew heavy as her figure faded in the distance.

He wanted to make her smile again. Wanted her to tease him. Wanted the joy bubble surrounding her to include him.

If he moved here…would she be happy about it?

He plucked a blade of grass and wound it in his fingers. He'd be financially unstable. Taking a risk—a risk that might not pay off. It would take all of his substantial savings to invest in real estate. What would everyone think if Reed set up a construction firm only to fail?

And what about Dad? They'd texted a few times since getting ice cream. Would moving here ruin the bud of their relationship?

Reed bent his good leg and rested his elbow on his knee. All of those questions didn't concern him as much as the one he'd been avoiding.

Could he make a commitment to Claire? He wouldn't have a solid job. What if he failed and needed to move? He couldn't ask her to do that. She loved her family too much. And, frankly, he doubted she'd move, not if given a choice between Lake Endwell and him.

He inadvertently caused friction in families. Why did he imagine it would be different with Claire's?

He had too much to lose to be toying with the idea of moving to Lake Endwell.

Chapter Fourteen

Another Saturday night with nothing to do, no one to see and a wicked mood to match. Wearing shorts and a navy blue T-shirt, Claire became one with her couch, eating a bowl of mint chocolate chip ice cream, watching a mind-numbing hour of *CSI*.

She'd barely spoken to Reed since Thursday night. The fireworks had been lovely, but the entire time they flashed in the sky, she'd wanted to take Reed's hand and encourage him to think about moving here. For a brief moment during the fireworks finale she thought he was going to kiss her. He'd taken her hand in his, but he let it go. Since then they'd fallen into an odd, tense place—and she missed their laid-back friendship.

Did she scare him? He'd been clear about his anxieties regarding families. Not that she understood his fears. Not really.

He had texted her yesterday. Dale and I are checking progress on bakery. Won't be home until late.

Shoving the spoon in her mouth, she licked the ice cream off. Contemplated chucking the utensil across the room.

What had she expected? Reed to only work with her?

Reed stayed to help with the rebuilding efforts. He'd said nothing about staying for her.

Her chest tightened. Why had she allowed herself to get so close to him? He wasn't exactly available. Sure, he was single, but he lived in another state.

And he cared more about stupid roofs and drywall than her.

This time she did chuck the spoon across the room, enjoying the sound of it clattering against her hardwood floor. *Real mature, Claire.*

Reed was returning to Chicago in a few days. And she had less than two weeks left with her otters.

Today she'd spent hours at the zoo, checking the new facilities. Tina's second cousin had been there too, and he seemed awfully comfortable with the staff. Joking, checking the charts, offering to grab Tina a coffee. Bile climbed up Claire's throat. What could she do? Tina had stopped her earlier to let her know the staff would be making a decision within the week. Either Claire's credentials were enough, or Mr. Charismatic Cousin would get the job.

Claire plodded to her bedroom and grabbed her laptop. Time to create a backup plan. Just in case.

In case what? Reed left? He'd planned on it all along.

Duh. That wasn't the issue. This was about her job. J.O.B. Not R.E.E.D.

She checked on the vet technician positions in southwest Michigan. Of the three she'd found last week, only two were still available. And the pay would be low, but she didn't need the money all that much. With the cottage almost paid for and her stake in Sheffield Auto, she could afford to take a low-paying job. She typed a search for jobs…and she peeled herself off the couch to find a pad of paper and a pen. There were some real possibilities—if she relocated.

Tapping the pen against her chin, she let the Chicago

idea permeate. Yeah, she could take the Lake Michigan beaches. The yummy pizza. The killer shopping.

Reed.

The pen slipped from her hand.

Chicago sounded good, but it would never do. Her throat seized at the thought of not seeing Dad and Libby and Aunt Sally every day. No dinners at Uncle Joe's? Impossible.

She'd find a backup job around here or none at all.

Her phone dinged. She lunged for it, hating how her pulse pounded in hope. She read the message, her shoulders falling.

Tommy.

Tigers game at our house. Bring chips and dip.

Her Saturday night just got better. Baseball. Her brothers. Yay.

"I haven't been this excited since I took woodshop in high school," Dale said. "This is a solid plan. You could make it work."

Reed met Dale's proud gaze across the table at Pat's Diner. Red vinyl covered the seats of the booth, and outside, small American flags waved next to the flowers in planters. The aroma of french fries filled the air.

"I'm still trying it on for size." Reed flicked his fingers toward the pile of papers he'd handwritten yesterday. His hastily drawn up business plan. He'd tried to ignore the idea. Tried to stay excited about the vice president position. And he'd failed. "I don't know if I'll go through with it."

"Listen, son, now is the time to start a construction firm around here. We lost half a dozen builders when the market crashed. Demand's picked up. You have the knowledge. You already have a good reputation. If you need financial backing, I'll stand behind you."

Reed forgot to exhale. Dale's generosity shocked him. "It means a lot to me—more than you know—but I don't need financing. I've saved a lot of money over the years."

Dale gave him a shy look. "What about a superintendent?"

Superintendent? Reed hadn't thought that far. He figured—*if* he went through with it—he would run the business on his own until it was profitable enough to hire someone. He pushed the papers to the side. "I'll have to hire someone eventually. Got someone in mind for the job?"

"Me."

Reed frowned, unsure what Dale was saying. "You mean you'll help me hire someone?"

"No. I mean I want the job."

Reed thought about it, flipped it around, studied the angles.

"I might not have a license or professional training," Dale said. "But I know this town. I've been a backyard warrior for forty years, building decks, repairing roofs, helping with wiring."

Dale. The ideal superintendent. But why? "Anyone would hire you in a minute, but you don't really want the job, do you?"

"I know it sounds crazy. Maybe it is crazy. I didn't realize how useless I felt. I finally found a purpose helping you organize the reconstruction efforts." Dale tapped his knuckles on the table. "I didn't get to choose my vocation. I've always been grateful to take over my dad's dealerships. Never had to worry about money a day in my life. I raised my kids here and passed the business to my boys. Would have to the girls too, but they weren't interested."

"What about the dealerships?" Reed asked. "You still play an active role in them."

Dale leaned back. "Sheffield Auto practically runs itself. It was more stressful before Tommy and Bryan came on board. Sam might be coming over too. He's finishing his master's degree in business management."

The idea of working with Dale every day appealed to Reed. They got along well, had settled into a comfortable rhythm. Dale had a knack for following up on project details Reed didn't have time for, ones that could hold up the next phase of construction.

"I'm bored." Dale stared out the window, his profile serious. "Until you showed up, I went through my days on autopilot, always ready for something to fix. I didn't realize I could do more than weekend projects. Watching these buildings get new life reignited my passion. We only have so many years on this earth. I don't want to spend the rest of them bumbling along. I want to do what I want to do."

Reed picked up his coffee mug. "I don't know what to say."

"Don't say anything. Think about it. And for the record, I'm a wealthy man. I won't work for free, but I would defer a paycheck until you get your feet wet. Say a year."

Every drop of tension dissipated from Reed's body. This man had shown him nothing but kindness since the day Reed arrived. And now Dale was offering to work with him? Without pay?

That kind of faith in him—in Reed Hamilton the man, not the employee—he hadn't experienced before, and he liked how it felt, wanted to live up to the faith Claire's dad had in him.

"Like I said, keep it in mind." Dale twined his fingers together and rested them on the table. "You don't have to rush anything. We sure would like to see more of you here, though, whatever you decide."

Reed still had a lot of unanswered questions of the what-if variety, but he believed Dale.

"Come on." Dale grabbed the bill for their coffees and

slid out of the booth. "Let's watch the Tigers on Tommy's big screen."

Another night without Claire? Reed should text her. See if she wanted to come too. He hadn't seen her since the fireworks on Thursday. If only they could return to their easy banter. He'd give about anything to get their comfortable relationship back.

But what if Dale told her about the business plan? Reed frowned. And what if she told him in no uncertain terms she didn't like the idea? He didn't want the conversation played out in front of her brothers.

He'd wait. Call her tomorrow.

Tomorrow seemed a long time away.

Stupid chips and dip.

Claire plodded down aisle three of Lake Endwell Grocery, her flip-flops slapping against the linoleum. She should have stayed home. She didn't even like baseball. Surely she could have found an old romantic comedy on television or rented something. Anything.

A sale on potato chips caught her eye. Loved the taste, but this brand lacked the heft to properly dip. She moved farther down. The other brand had thicker ridges, but— she narrowed her eyes as she lifted the bag—the manufacturers put, like, six chips in and pumped the rest with air.

With a bag in each hand, she tried to figure out which held more chips.

What was she doing? She'd hit a new low, wasting time in the snack aisle at the grocery store. Grabbing two of each, she moved to the candy aisle and snatched four packages of M&M's, a giant pack of Skittles and two Tootsie Pops for good measure. If she was going to sit through a game at her loud brothers' house, she needed sugar and lots of it.

She dropped her loot on the express-lane counter and glanced up—and wished she hadn't.

Tammy and Mark. Dressed up for a night to remember, from the looks of them. Tammy's smile slid away as she eyed Claire. Mark dismissed Claire with a quick turn of his head. "I'll be right back."

A teenage kid scanned the first item from her mound of junk food.

Why now? Why did she have to run into these two when all signs pointed to her being on some sort of eating binge?

"Claire. Good to see you." Tammy slowly perused her selections.

Be nice. "You're dressed up. Big plans tonight?"

A blush rose to Tammy's cheeks. She lowered her gaze, then met Claire's. "Actually, yes. Mark just proposed." Tammy thrust her hand out, revealing the huge sparkling diamond on a simple gold band.

Claire's heart swan-dived and landed on the floor with a splat.

Of course. Tammy and Mark.

A proposal, a wedding, a forever with the man she loved.

Clarity filled her head.

Claire wanted it too.

She loved Reed. She wanted forever with him.

Lifting her head high, Claire took a deep breath. "Congratulations."

Tammy seemed to be fighting emotions. Claire didn't care—time to round up her load of calories and sprint out the door.

"Thanks." Tammy shifted her weight from one spike-heeled strappy sandal to the other. "Well, I'll see you around."

"That'll be $21.59."

Rummaging through her purse, Claire found her credit

card and handed it to the kid. Accepted her bags. And left without another word.

In the safety of her car, she pounded the steering wheel with her fist. Why did she have to run into them tonight? At least Mark hadn't lingered. She'd avoided having to speak with him. But Tammy...

Her ex-boss really *had* looked beautiful. The ring really *had* sparkled.

Claire blinked away tears. She and Tammy had gotten along so well at first. They'd been friends. And now, instead of being genuinely happy for Tammy, Claire resented her. Resented how Tammy had shut off their friendship because of a guy. Still couldn't get past the injustice of being fired.

A tear slipped down her cheek, and she angrily flicked it away. It was stupid to be this upset. So they were getting married. It didn't involve her.

Her eyes welled with tears. If it didn't involve her, why did it bother her so much?

Because I've been wearing my bitterness, and it's heavy. I resent Mark for spreading rumors about me. I'm mad at Tammy for firing me. I still blame Justin for my life not turning out the way I wanted it to.

She took a deep breath and wiped her eyes. Yes, Tammy had fired her, but losing her job had allowed Claire to help Reed with rebuilding the town. And who cared if Mark told lies about her? Claire never liked him much anyhow. As for Justin...

She stared ahead as cars pulled in and out of the parking lot.

Lord, please forgive me for the anger and bitterness I've been clinging to.

Something pressed on her heart. Asking for forgiveness from God was a start, but she too needed to forgive.

Could she? Tears threatened again. Oh, how it hurt.

Help me say this and mean it, dear Jesus, You who spared nothing for me.

She dropped her head in her hands.

Forgive them all. Bless Tammy and Mark's marriage. And take care of Justin too.

There. She felt empty. Lighter. For the first time in years, living somewhere other than Lake Endwell didn't sound terrible. Maybe Chicago wasn't that bad. Not bad at all.

Chapter Fifteen

"What are you talking about, Dad?" The planes of Tommy's face sharpened as he glowered at Dale, then at Reed. Bryan appeared equally stunned from the other recliner. The announcers on TV laughed before discussing the one-two pitch.

Reed closed his eyes, inwardly groaning. Why had Dale blurted out his unofficial and unlikely-to-happen plan? At least Claire wasn't here—that would be a nightmare.

Unaffected by the tension sizzling in the room, Dale rocked back and forth on his heels. "Reed moving to Lake Endwell. I think it's a good idea."

The vein in Tommy's temple pulsed. "That's not what I meant and you know it."

"What's the problem, then?" Dale crossed his arms over his chest.

"The problem?" Tommy snorted with a shake of his head. "You've run Sheffield Auto forever, and now you want to quit? I think you've lost your mind."

Dale cocked his head to the side. "I haven't lost anything. I've found it. You and Bryan have been running the day-to-day operations for years. What's the big deal?"

"I can't believe you." Tommy waved his hand, dismissing the topic. "I don't know what to say."

"You're the CEO," Bryan said. "Who is going to step in and run it?"

"One of you can," Dale said.

Tommy and Bryan both looked at their father as if he'd grown pink pigtails.

"We don't want to run it," they said in unison.

Dale stepped back, his face falling. "What? Why?"

"I have my hands full with my dealerships." Tommy raked his hand through his hair. "I don't want to make company decisions too. I want a life."

"It's not that time-consuming," Dale said. "I go in for a couple hours in the afternoon and I'm done. You two practically run the company as it is."

Bryan drummed his fingers against his thigh. "I don't want the responsibility. I'm not going to be the one who runs Granddad's company into the ground. Why do you want to do construction anyway? What brought this on?"

"Yeah, is this some sort of midlife crisis?"

Reed's gut heaved as the argument heated up. He had never intended to divide their family. He hadn't planned on involving their family at all until Dale suggested it. This was becoming an explosive mess. *Way to go, Reed. Still got that special touch.*

"I'd better leave," Reed said.

"No, Reed. Stay." Dale held his palms out. "Maybe it *is* a midlife crisis. I don't know. I'm restless. Bored of pushing papers around, checking on investments and calling it a life. If either of you doesn't like your job, you can quit. No one ever said you had to work for the family."

Tommy's face reddened. "I don't want to quit! Why would you even say that? This is about you quitting. Not me." He pivoted and stalked to the kitchen.

The front door opened and Claire, carrying bulging plastic bags, entered.

This couldn't be happening.

Reed dug his fingernails into his palms.

Had she been crying? Some of her hair escaped a loose ponytail, her face was flushed and her posture defeated. Reed moved toward her.

"Great." Bryan threw his hands up. "Let's find out what Claire thinks. Don't tell me you're going along with this?"

Reed halted. Bryan was going to blab everything. Here. In front of Claire.

"What do I think about what? Here, take these." She pushed the bags to him and slipped her flip-flops off.

Everything in Reed wanted to go to her, to curl his arms around her waist, pick her up and whisk her out of there. To explain. But his heart had stopped beating a minute ago.

This night would get worse before it got better.

Claire threw him a sharp glance. Reed's muscles tensed.

Bryan moved the bags to his other hand. "Reed's opening a construction firm here and wants Dad to be the superintendent."

Her face drained of color. Reed took another step. "Nothing is concrete. I *might* be opening a business—"

Dale nodded. "And I mentioned I *wanted* to be the super. You two got ahead of me. Reed and I are just talking about it."

Claire faced her dad. "What about Sheffield Auto?"

"That's what I said." Tommy barreled back in. "Can you believe this?"

A flush crept up Dale's neck. "You're all making a big fuss about nothing. If no one wants to step up and run the company, I'll still do it. I'll do both. We'll discuss it later." He turned to Reed. "I'm sorry, son. Didn't know I was starting a war."

Reed almost corrected him. Dale wasn't the one starting a war. Reed was. It was always him.

On cue, the door opened and Libby, Jake and Sam filled the small entrance. Reed couldn't tear his gaze from Claire.

"Looks like we're missing a party," Sam said. "Hope you have food. I'm starving."

Tommy proceeded to fill Sam in on the conversation, but Reed didn't listen. He longed to go to Claire, to pull her aside. But she'd captured his gaze a minute ago and hadn't stopped staring, accusing.

How could he explain? *I didn't mean to hurt your family, Claire. I thought this time might be different.*

He opened his mouth to speak, but she cut him off with a jerky shake of her head.

"What's the big deal?" Sam shrugged. "If Dad wants to quit and you two are happy running the dealerships, I'll oversee the rest. It's not like Dad won't show me the ropes. If I have questions, he's right here."

"Now, wait a second!" Tommy bellowed.

"You don't know what you're doing." Bryan rolled his eyes.

"Stop it!" Dale thrust his hands out. "I didn't raise you to be disrespectful to each other, and you're being rude to Reed."

Reed couldn't stand here any longer. This plan would never work. Claire and her brothers resented him. Her big blue eyes had filled with tears, and her face grew paler by the minute. He wouldn't wrench their family apart—not for any reason.

He stomped his crutch on the floor to get their attention. "I'm not starting a business here. I'm going back to Chicago." He closed the distance to Claire, searched her eyes and took her hand in his. "I'm sorry, Claire."

Her lips trembled. A tear slipped down her cheek.

He deserved this. He shouldn't have stayed. And he should have confided in her about the business before talking to Dale. To have her witness the chaos he inflicted on families? Cruel. No wonder she stared at him as if he'd kidnapped one of her otters.

"Jake, would you take me home?"

Jake nodded.

"Reed, wait." Dale came up to them. "I should have spoken to the boys privately—I didn't know they would go crazy. Don't go—they'll cool down."

"No, I'm the one in the wrong. Forget I ever brought up the idea." And Reed left.

Claire dug her fingers into the edge of Tommy's unmade bed, her knee bouncing, and stared unseeing out the window. She'd befriended Reed, taken care of him and, against her better judgment, gotten close. Pretended this time would be different. That she wouldn't get hurt. What did she know?

"Claire?"

She straightened. Libby sat beside her, the bed creaking under her weight.

"Why aren't you trying to convince Reed to stay?" Libby tipped her head to the side.

Why was Libby so perceptive? Although it didn't take a lot of analytical skills after her reaction back there. Weariness climbed up Claire's body, pressing on her tight shoulders.

"I wouldn't be the reason he's staying." Claire trailed a finger along the wrinkled sheet. She let out a mirthless laugh.

"I'm not following you." Libby slipped her arm around Claire and squeezed. "What happened?"

"I don't know. One minute we're having dinner at Granddad's cottage, and the next Reed's making me laugh and we're working together and talking all the time…" She bit her lip, not wanting to continue. Not knowing how to continue.

"And you might be a little bit in love with him," Libby said.

"How dumb can I be? I'm tired of being so optimistic about life. I've got to start seeing the world the way it is—not the way I want it to be."

Reed hadn't considered staying for her, and he hadn't bothered to confide in her. How hard would it be to say, "Hey, Claire, guess what? I'm thinking of starting a business"?

Duped. Again. With nobody but herself to blame.

The fact that he'd told Dad and her brothers before her? Humiliating.

All the time they'd spent together. All the laughter—the secrets—the kiss. Worthless.

"What am I going to do?" Claire dabbed her eyes, sniffling. "If I don't get the zoo job, I guess I'll sell Dad's cars or something. Looks like someone will have to."

"You couldn't do that!" Libby sounded horrified.

"I was kidding, Libs." She took a deep breath and tried to control her emotions.

"You'll get the zoo job. You will."

The whir of the ceiling fan blended with the muted voices of the men in the living room.

"Tommy still lives like a pig. Can't he make his bed once a season at least?" Libby smoothed the covers. "At least it doesn't smell in here, I guess."

Claire barked out a laugh. "Remember his football cleats? My word, they reeked."

"I remember. I'm still trying to forget." Libby chuckled, then sobered. "What if Reed changes his mind and moves to Lake Endwell?"

"He won't," Claire said. "You heard him."

"But what if—"

Claire rose, clenching her hands together. "It wouldn't matter. He wouldn't be doing it for me. It would be to start a business. Or to be near Jake. I don't know. But I'm not a factor in the deal."

She wasn't an everyday girl for Reed—she wasn't even a Tuesday girl. She was nobody. Maybe God's plan was for her to be alone. Forever.

"Reed hasn't visited Jake in years," Libby said. "He could start a business anywhere. You two grew close—anyone could see it. Reed is not the type of guy to move here without a good reason."

"Yeah, and I'm not the reason. He's not moving here, okay? Let's drop it."

"Now who's being uncompromising?" Libby asked. "Shouldn't you at least talk to him before you judge? That's what you and Aunt Sally are always telling me."

"We've barely spoken since the Fourth."

"Big whoop. Get everything out in the open before he leaves."

Libby was right. Claire hated it when she was right. "It's hard."

"Hey, I know it's hard. But it'll be worth it. You'll know where you stand."

"What if I don't want to know? Reality never lives up to my dreams."

A soft smile lifted Libby's lips. "Sometimes reality is better than your dreams."

Reed had been living in a fictional haze of his own making, thinking he could figure out how to have it all. He leaned on the crutches, the crescent moon casting a squiggly glow on the lake. What good was having it all if Claire hated him?

"You sure about this?" Jake flicked the outside lights on and stepped onto the deck at the cottage. "You don't have to go. Tommy and Bryan get hotheaded over everything. Two minutes later, they're back to normal. Don't take it personal."

"It's not them."

"What is it, then?" Jake stood next to him and leaned against the rail. "Dale? I can see why you might not want to work with him, but he has connections. He could help you get established here. Hey, it's your call."

"It's not Dale. I respect him. I'm dumbfounded he offered."

"He offered?" Jake sounded perplexed, peeved even.

"Yeah." Reed hopped on one foot to the lounge chair and carefully extended his cast on the cushion before setting his crutches down.

"Why would he want to work with *you*?" Jake towered over him.

Reed rubbed his forehead, ignoring his menacing brother. What was so bad about working with him?

"Sit down," Reed said. Tree branches rustled in the wind. "My neck is going to snap trying to stare at you."

Jake grunted, but he dragged a chair over and dropped into it. "I'm trying to figure out all this interest in you. Dale's always been friendly with me, but we don't exactly sit around talking all the time. I can think of maybe two occasions, tops."

"What are you trying to say, Jake? I'm stealing your future father-in-law? Come on!" Reed opened his hands. "Dale came over every day to help me with this cast because I couldn't do anything. Couldn't dress myself. Couldn't make a bowl of cereal those first days. We talked. We have a lot in common. I wasn't trying to come between you, if that's what you're saying."

No matter what Reed did, he found a way to mess up family dynamics, even between Jake and Dale.

Jake hung his head, his elbows propped on his knees. "I—maybe I'm jealous."

"Of Dale and me talking?"

"I don't know." Jake lowered his chin. "It's more than that. You're more than a big brother to me. But for some reason, we've never been real close. What does Dale have that I don't?"

Reed drew in a sharp breath. *How have I missed the obvious? Jake isn't jealous of Dale getting close to me. He's jealous of me getting close to someone other than him.*

"I'm sorry." Reed sighed. "I haven't been around, haven't been here for you and I'm sorry for that. It's never been you—I mean it."

Uncertainty shone in his eyes.

"Seriously, Jake, my mom's death messed me up. I lost my world—and I didn't want my new world. But I always wanted you. I've always been proud of you."

Jake's throat worked as he nodded. "I never cared about superheroes, Reed. You were it for me. I want you around. Do me a favor. Stick it out here a couple more nights. Everyone will calm down, change their attitudes. You'll see."

"I can't, Jake. It's more complicated than that."

"Why?"

"Because I'm in love with Claire."

Chapter Sixteen

"We have to talk." Claire marched up the ramp to Grand-dad's deck, ignoring Jake's and Reed's shocked expressions. Her nerves jangled more than the rows of silver bracelets Libby usually wore. "Jake, could you give us a minute?"

"I'll give you more than a minute. I'll give you all night. See ya, Reed. Call me tomorrow."

"Wait, Jake!" Reed fumbled to lift his crutches. Jake bounded down the ramp, and seconds later, an engine roared, followed by the crunch of tires on the short gravel drive.

"I almost didn't come here." She lifted her chin, trying to hold on to the bravado she'd worked up on the way over.

"I don't blame you." He attempted to stand.

"No, don't get up. Stay there." She sat in Jake's empty chair. Now what? She'd come over, but she didn't know what to say.

"I'm sorry, Claire." The sincerity in his expression lowered her anger a notch, but she held on, determined not to slink away before she made her point. He faced her, carefully setting his right foot on the deck. Shadows from the porch lights flitted about. "I should have told you. I planned on telling you. I didn't know how. Or when. Dale blurted it out before I could stop him."

"But why?" The hurt of being the last to know sprinted back. "We aren't exactly strangers, Reed. All you would have had to do is pick up the phone. Call me. Hey, a text would have been better than hearing it from my brothers." She tried, oh how she tried, to keep the accusation out of her tone, but it hung there, aimed, firing.

"I didn't want them to know!" Reed clenched his jaw and rotated his neck toward the lake. "I didn't want anyone to know. I was kicking an idea around, and out of the blue, your dad wants to join me. I was as shocked as anyone."

"Well, that makes me feel so much better. You didn't want anyone to know—including me. Fantastic." She wanted to stalk home, but there was more on the line here than her pride. A lot more.

"That's not what I meant."

"Are you sure?" she asked. "Dad might be high energy, but he's not impulsive. He wouldn't jump into something that wasn't well thought out, so don't try to convince me you haven't been thinking about this for a while."

Furrows grew deep between his eyebrows. "It's not like that. It's not."

"What is it, then? You obviously have been thinking about moving here, but you don't want me to know about it. And since you won't discuss it with me, I'm thinking I'm what's holding you back."

"How can you say that?" He seared her with stricken eyes. "It's not you. It's me."

She clamped her mouth shut and glared at him. Had he really given her such a lame line? *It's not you. It's me?* She should beat him over the head with his crutch. "Real original, Reed. I think everything's been said." She rose.

"Sit." He pointed to her chair, his face hard.

If her heart wasn't collapsing into a shriveled pile, she

might have come up with a clever comeback and found the energy to stomp out of there.

Reed's jaw tightened. "I'm thirty-three years old and I've never had a serious relationship with a woman. Ever."

She scooted back in her chair. This didn't sound promising.

"Don't get me wrong, I don't sit home on Saturday nights. I have no problem dating, but not long-term."

Was he trying to let her down gently with this speech? What exactly was he saying? He preferred short-term to long-term? A date-of-the-week rather than something real? She didn't care how cute he was or how amazing he kissed, she would never settle for less again.

He rubbed the back of his neck. "Coming here for the wedding was another two days to knock off my to-do list. I love Jake, want to see him happy, but I had no intention of hanging around. So when I had to stay, I tried to protect myself and get it over with."

"Protect yourself from what?" Her words slipped out.

"From getting hurt. Getting close to anyone. I mess things up with everyone I care for. After Dad and Barbara married, I moved on with life as best I could, and by high school, I finally felt good again. I spent more time at my best friend's house than my own. We had all kinds of plans for when we got out of school. Collin always said we were a team."

A team. She dreaded whatever he was about to say.

"I should have known better," he said. "Nothing lasts. Three months before we graduated, Collin got caught with marijuana. He got expelled."

"Oh, no." Claire brought her hand to her chest. "And there went your plans."

He nodded, a bitter movement. "And my best friend. Collin put all the blame on me. Told his parents the drugs were mine. That I set him up to keep from getting in trouble."

"They believed him?"

"Yeah. The principal searched my locker but didn't find any evidence. Didn't matter. Collin's parents told me to stay away from him. I never talked to him again. Dad, Barbara and Jake moved to Lake Endwell a few months later."

So much of what Reed had told her over the past month made sense. Why he feared getting close. Why he avoided families. He'd been the scapegoat of his mom's family and his best friend's parents.

"No questions?" Reed blinked. "No 'did you set him up? Did you smoke pot with him?'"

"No." The tension in her shoulders eased. "You're loyal. You do what you say you're going to. I don't know if you smoked with him, but I do know you didn't set him up."

"What if I told you I did?"

A heavy silence fell.

"Then I'd say you made a mistake and God forgave you. But I don't believe you did."

"I didn't. I would never deliberately hurt someone close to me." He stood, held his hand out and when she placed hers in it, he wrapped his arms around her, crushing her to his chest. "I just—I needed to know what you would say." He pressed his lips to the top of her head. "Your faith in me—I can't tell you what it means."

She clung to him, the rapid beat of his heart loud in her ears, and she breathed in his cologne, holding on tightly. Anything to prolong the moment.

"I know you're afraid of losing another family," she said. "If you moved here, it wouldn't be like that."

"It already is. Even Dad and Barbara—I've been the thorn in our family since they got married. I ruin relationships."

"Your dad and Barbara are happy together. How could you think you ruined anything?"

Reed averted his eyes. "I create the tension. I'm the one who makes everyone uncomfortable when we're together."

"Families are full of tension—it's just how they are."

"You saw what happened at your brothers' house. I'm not going to be a wedge, driving your brothers and dad apart. They'll resent me—they already do—and you will too."

"They'll get over it," Claire said.

"They won't have to. I'm leaving."

Claire's soul sank.

His gaze bored into hers, burning, reaching, begging. "I care about you, Claire. You...you make me want to stay."

She wrung her hands.

"I love you." He touched her cheek.

Her lungs locked—she couldn't exhale. He loved her? But he still planned on leaving?

"I love you too." Claire drew her shoulders back. "But I don't know what you want, and I'm not sure of you. I can't be the Tuesday girl again."

"You're not a—"

She put her finger to his lips. "My entire adult life, I've waited for life to treat me fairly. I thought if I worked hard enough, my bosses would reward me. If I was the perfect girlfriend and waited patiently at home, my Prince Charming would snatch me up. Well, guess what? I was wrong. I never demanded anything, but this time I'm going to. I'm demanding something, okay?" She hitched her chin, looked him in the eyes and took a deep breath. "You say you love me, but I will never be content with being the last to know about your life. I want to be the first to know everything. Your fears. Your dreams. Your plans."

"You're the person I want to tell everything to." Reed's eyes pleaded with her. "I reach for my phone ten times a day. I *want* to tell you everything."

"Then why don't you?" She scrunched her forehead, trying to understand.

"What if I move here and start a construction firm and it fails? Or what if your dad becomes my superintendent and your brothers hate me forever? What if this—this attraction, this thing we have between us—goes away in three months? I've spent the last twenty years in awkward silence with my dad. I don't want to go through that with you too. I can't move here, Claire. There's too much for me to lose."

She held her breath, her insides ready to burst. She got it. He loved her, but his fears prevented him from living in Lake Endwell. He thought he was protecting her by staying away. What could she say to change his mind?

"I love you too, Reed." She took both his hands in hers. "I love you, and we can work this out."

His eyes blazed. "I still have to go. It doesn't change anything. I've messed up enough lives. I'm not messing up yours."

"You have it backward." Hope and fear braided through her body. "They were the ones who ruined yours." She closed the gap between them, threading her arms around his waist.

He tipped her chin up. And he kissed her. Slow, long, he stole her breath, and she sank into him, giving him whatever he needed, trying to convey how much she cared.

With a raggedy breath, she broke off the kiss. "Don't go, Reed."

"I love you," Reed whispered, his hands at the back of her neck, fingers in her hair. "I love you more than anything."

His heart plummeted. This dark-haired beauty with the mesmerizing eyes and passionate heart had unknowingly sealed the door on his decision. He couldn't stay. He would hurt her—somehow he would cause her pain. And it was preventable. Claire meant too much to him.

"I have to go. You know it. I know it. I can't stay."

Her face paled. "What happens to us?"

"I don't know."

"There's nothing I can say to convince you, is there?"

Regret burned inside him. "No."

"I'm not enough to make you stay," she said, under her breath. Then she lifted a too-bright smile, so full of regret it sliced his heart open. "Say no more."

She turned and walked away. As her figure retreated into the darkness, Reed fought not to follow her. What good would it do? She *was* enough for him—hadn't he just told her he loved her? He was leaving for her sake. For his sake.

He frowned.

For whose sake?

Chapter Seventeen

Reed shoved four fries in his mouth as Dad merged onto the highway the next day. Other than a few sentences of small talk, the ride to the airport had been silent. Big surprise. Dad took a long drink from a large Coke and exhaled.

"That good, huh?" Reed couldn't resist asking.

"Fountain pop tastes the best."

Reed took another bite of his burger. Should he tackle the fifty-foot-tall elephant or not? It had been in the room with them for so many years. Maybe he should let it stand.

But the deep green of the trees against the bright blue sky, so similar to the view he'd enjoyed from Claire's family cottage, triggered the peace Reed had found and lost this summer.

It was time.

Time to settle the gnawing uncertainty that ate at him in his father's presence. Time to try.

"What's wrong with us?" Reed kept his tone light.

Dad's hands tightened on the steering wheel.

"I—" Reed continued. "I wish we could work this out. I want to have a normal conversation with you. One where we can talk without the awkward thing we have going."

The muscle in Dad's cheek flickered, as if twenty years had bottled up, ready to explode. Maybe they had.

"It was my fault." Dad's words marched out. "You know it. I know it. I look at you and I know I failed."

Reed almost dropped his half-eaten burger. "What are you talking about?" A round of explanations came to mind. All negative. His stomach dipped. Maybe he shouldn't have eaten a bunch of greasy fries right before this conversation. Maybe he shouldn't have initiated it either.

"You want to talk about it?" Dad asked. "Now? After all this time?"

"Yes." No. Maybe. What exactly were they talking about?

"It was my fault your mother died. End of story."

"Um, whoa, what?" Reed's incredulous tone was too loud. He lowered his voice. "If that's the end, you're going to have to share the beginning and the middle, because I don't know any of it."

He shot Reed a sad glance. "You do. I wish I could have been a better dad, but how do you look at your own son and know you destroyed his life? I thought Barbara was what you needed. She made me feel good. I thought you'd feel the same. But I messed up again. Thinking of myself."

"Back up—way up," Reed said. "You didn't ruin my life. Why would you think that?"

Surprise lifted his eyebrows. "You sound like you mean it."

"I do mean it. *I* was the problem. I couldn't figure out how to fit in anymore."

"I should have done things differently," Dad said. "I didn't have a clue. I was lost, wading around, grabbing for answers and coming up empty."

"Dad?"

"Yeah?"

"Tell me what happened. With Mom."

Dad trained his eyes on the road. "I should have stopped her. That night, and before. She didn't start drinking until you were out of diapers. Must have been around three or four. She'd have a glass of wine at dinner. A vodka tonic in the afternoon. It was the third miscarriage that did it. She didn't hide the bottles anymore."

Three babies? Reed's mind reeled. He had assumed his mom was depressed. She was never happy or even hot-tempered like his friends' moms. She was just kind of there. A pat on his head when he got home from school and a slurred "sweet boy" on the good days. On the bad ones, he wouldn't see her, just the back of her bedroom door.

"Your grandmother told me I had to remove all the liquor from the house, and I did. But Meredith snuck it in. We fought a lot. I guess I hoped she'd snap out of it. I knew all her secret stashes, tossed everything out. She still found booze. When her family decided to confront her, I didn't think it would help."

Empathy for Dad poured over him. "I never knew you were dealing with all that."

"Well," Dad said, "I tried to protect you."

"Did they do it? Confront her?"

The most lost look Reed had ever seen crumpled his dad's face. Reed longed to reach over and put his hand on Dad's shoulder, tell him it was all right, but he didn't dare. Not before he heard it all.

"They came over to our house," Dad said. "They were waiting in the living room for her, like a surprise party but without anything to celebrate, you know. I told them she would know something was up when she saw the cars. She'd been shopping with a girlfriend all day—at least that's what she told me."

How had he not realized Dad grappled with so much guilt? No wonder they'd been unable to string more than five sentences of conversation together since the funeral.

"I should have told them no." Dad pressed the heel of his hand into the steering wheel. "Should have made her go to AA. Should have taken my stupid head out of the sand long enough to know it wasn't working. I should have done a lot of things. She stumbled through the front door, stopped, took them all in. Aunts, uncles, siblings and finally your grandmother. Meredith's glazed-over eyes and swaying posture told me what I should have known— she'd lied about shopping. Any fool could see she'd been drinking all day."

"What'd she do?"

"She left. Without a word." Dad shrugged, his jaw revealing anger rather than guilt. "I was furious. I knew she was in no shape to drive, but I'd had it. The lying, the hiding, the empty bottles everywhere. I wanted her to leave. I didn't want to deal with it—with her—anymore."

"Is that the night she died?"

He nodded, his knuckles white against the wheel. "I'm sorry, Reed. I should have gone after her. Stopped her. Maybe you'd still have a mother if I had been a better husband."

Reed's throat tightened, sympathy pressing against the backs of his eyes. "It wasn't your fault."

His jaw tensed. "They blamed me."

"How could they blame you?"

"I'll never forget the hatred in her eyes when she pointed her finger at me and said, 'You did this. You should have stopped her. She would be alive right now if you had done something.'"

Reed jerked his head back. "Who? Why would anyone say that to you?"

"Your grandmother. She never talked to me again. Didn't talk to you either. I…I thought it would be better for both of us if we moved. The kids at school were gossiping, and, well, you were asking questions about the family. Why didn't they visit anymore? Why didn't anyone come over for your birthday? Why did Grandma ignore you when you saw her at the store? I was tired of the bad memories. Wanted a new start for both of us."

Reed tried to process everything as his breathing grew short and raspy. Why hadn't he figured this out before? Why, with every word ringing true, was this such a shock?

"I wish you had told me all this a long time ago. I thought—well, I thought I reminded you of Mom and you didn't want to remember. That I'd done something wrong for the family to cut things off with me. I blamed myself for Mom dying, for losing the family, for having to move."

"You had nothing to blame yourself for." His gruff words were full of conviction. "You were a kid. Innocent."

"But I didn't know that," Reed said, his voice rising.

His dad sighed. "I thought you blamed me the way the others did. I felt bad all the time. I wanted to forget it and move on."

"With Barbara," Reed said.

"Yeah."

"And you did."

"I did."

Reed slumped, bringing his knuckle to his lips, and stared mindlessly out the window. "I'm glad you did. Barbara is a nice woman. One of the nicest I've ever met."

"She is." He shot Reed another glance. "Why do you hate her?"

Reed clenched his jaw. He deserved that one. "I don't. I resented her. Maybe I still resent her."

"She never tried to be your mother."

"I know," Reed said. "That's not why."

"Spell it out for me." A field with tall cornstalks waved them on.

"You were comfortable with her," Reed said. "You weren't comfortable with me."

He slapped the wheel. "That was it?" And then Dad laughed. Loud. Long. "Here I thought… I've been pretty dumb. I had no idea."

Reed shrugged. "Well, now you know."

"Now I know."

"I lost everything when Mom died," Reed said quietly. "In a lot of ways, I lost you too."

Dad's chin trembled. "I want to make it up to you. I've always been proud of you, Reed. I hope you know that. I didn't know how to tell you. Didn't know how to show it."

The tough layers around Reed's heart peeled away. "We need a do over, don't we?"

"Yeah," Dad said shyly. "A do over. But first, I need you to do one thing for me."

Reed wanted to let go of the years of anger and disappointment. He'd wanted to for a long time. His decision balanced on the request. "What is it?"

"Forgive me."

Those two words ripped down his soul, and he had to bite his lip to keep the threatening tears back. If Dad had any idea how much those words meant to him… "I forgive you."

He cupped his hand on Reed's shoulder and squeezed it. Reed shook his head in wonder—the gesture he'd wanted to comfort Dad with had been given to him instead. Funny how life worked.

They drove in silence several minutes.

"Reed?"

"Yeah?"

"Would you prefer we spend time together without Barbara around?"

Reed's mind stilled. He used to want nothing more than alone time with Dad. No Barbara. But now?

"No." Reed shook his head. "I owe Barbara an apology, Dad. It's time we all got used to spending time together."

"You mean it?" His face brightened.

"Yeah. She's been patient with me for—" Reed ran his hand through his hair "—well, for as long as I've known her. You're fortunate to have her. I am too."

"You don't know how relieved I am to hear that. She'll be happy. She's always had a soft spot for you."

Reed's stomach dropped. Barbara had loved him when he didn't deserve it, and she continued to love him. He still didn't deserve it.

"Listen, if you change your mind about Chicago and want to start that business, you'll stay with us. You get around pretty good on those things. We'll take care of you."

The words fell like a shower on his parched heart. A family—his family—to rely on, to be part of?

Thank You, God. I lost my world back there, but I gained my dad.

"Claire, it's Tina. Congratulations, you got the job. Call me back when you get a chance and we'll go over the paperwork. Thrilled to have you on board full-time."

Oddly numb, Claire tossed her purse on the table but ended the voice mail and kept her cell phone in hand. She got the job.

Big deal.

It had been five days since she last saw Reed. Four days and twenty-one hours to be exact. After she left him Saturday night, she'd retreated into her house and sat in a trance.

What had gone wrong? He loved her. Love meant spinning in circles, being giddy, ecstatic.

Not her. Five days of heartbreak. Of loneliness. Emptiness.

Every day she went over what she could have done differently. What she could have said to change his mind. If she had tried harder, reasoned with him, kissed him one more time…

But he'd left. Libby told her his dad took him to the airport Sunday morning. And Jake drove Reed's truck back to him yesterday. Reed was gone. And so was her heart.

Claire swiped a Diet Coke from the fridge and went out back to play with Hansel and Gretel. She had just over a week left with them. They were moving to the zoo next Friday.

She took a sip. What was Reed doing now? She should have convinced him to move past his fears. Assured him he would always have a place in her family. He was a good man who didn't deserve the treatment he'd received.

Had she picked up the phone twenty times a day to call him? Yes.

Did she still check her phone fifty times a day for messages? Uh-huh.

She flopped onto a lawn chair and took a long drink from the pop. Hansel and Gretel raced to her, and she patted each of their heads before tossing them fruit slices.

"Claire? Are you home?"

Claire groaned. Aunt Sally pushed through the gate and joined her. "I'm worried about you."

"Come right out and tell me how you feel, why don't you?" Claire flung another apple slice to Gretel.

"You look like you haven't slept in a month. And you're wearing that awful fair T-shirt from five years ago. Goodwill wouldn't even take it at this point." Aunt Sally shook her head, her frosted pink lips puckered. "Even your brothers and Libby are concerned."

"Tell them to mind their own business. I'm fine." Claire had successfully avoided their calls and texts. She didn't want to listen to their lectures, gripes or whatever they had to say.

"You call this fine?" Sally's charm bracelet slipped down to her wrist with a tinkling noise. "You're in love."

"So?" Claire lifted one shoulder.

"So, you're in love and you're miserable, and the man you're in love with is gone. Does he love you? No, don't answer that."

Good, because she didn't want to answer. Thinking about it made her lower lip tremble. She would not cry. Not here. Not in front of Aunt Sally and the otters.

"I know he loves you," Sally said. "It was written all over his handsome face."

Claire bit the inside of her cheek, trying to curb the welling emotions within. Reed *did* have a handsome face.

"If you love him, and he loves you, why are you sitting in this backyard while he's somewhere else?"

"What do you mean?" Claire asked.

"I mean—" Sally widened her eyes "—do you want more than this or not?"

Claire rotated to take in her yellow cottage, the deck Dad built, the flowers spilling out from planters, the fenced yard, the gurgling pond and the otters chasing each other in the sunshine. Did she want more than this?

"I love my life," Claire said. The words lacked conviction.

"I know you used to love it, but can you still say that now that you've met Reed?"

Claire gripped the can. For years she'd thanked the Lord for all her blessings. She'd been given enough and she'd been content with what she had. But now...

Lord, I didn't ask for more, but I got it. And then I lost it. What do You want from me? Is this Your plan? Staying in Lake Endwell, working at the zoo and being with my family? Or are You trying to tell me something else?

Aunt Sally leaned her forearms on the back of the chair opposite Claire. "I talked to Libby and Dale. From what I can tell, Reed's been a loner for a long, long time. Maybe being around our close family is too hard for him. Plus, he has a successful job and might not want to give it up.

Expecting him to come here, well, it might be unrealistic on your part. If you love him and want to be with him, you're going to have to decide what's more important to you—staying here where everything is comfortable or taking a risk on Reed."

Claire sat up straight. "I am comfortable here. I've always been comfortable here. It's home. It's close to my loved ones."

"But you have a new loved one now, and it's not close to him."

"That's the problem. He has this ridiculous theory that he drives families apart." She leaned back, defeated. "Like he left for my benefit. I don't think so."

"Maybe he has a good reason to believe that, hon."

"But he wouldn't give me a chance."

"You sound like your sister. Unreasonable. Are you scared of *not* being with your family?" Aunt Sally pointed at her. "Think about it."

Chapter Eighteen

The view of Chicago's skyscrapers was usually spectac-
ular on a clear morning, but Reed barely glanced at it. He
hadn't been able to enjoy much of anything—not the trip
to Denver with John, not finding out they landed the hospital project, not even getting his cast off yesterday. His
leg was pale and thin, but he'd ditched the crutches. His
life was back.

His life *was* back...in Lake Endwell with Claire.

Two weeks had felt like eternity.

Stop thinking about her.

She wanted more from him. Wanted him to create a
new life there. She'd confessed her love and stuck to her
guns. He'd told her he loved her, but did she believe him?
Didn't she see he had to leave? That he would do anything
to keep from hurting her?

Reed propped his feet on the coffee table. She wanted
to be first. He wanted the same. A few calls and texts
wouldn't be enough for him either.

Swinging his legs around, he perched on the edge of the
couch with his head in his hands. The only person who was
happy about Reed being back was John. And Reed didn't
have the heart to confide in him. What would he say? *You
know that vice president title I've jabbered on about non-*

stop for years? Well, turns out I don't really want it after all. You understand, right?

Not even close.

He'd gotten calls from Dale, urging him to reconsider. Dale apologized for the drama and told him he was sorry he ever mentioned being Reed's superintendent, that he didn't realize his kids would put up a fight. He wanted Reed to come back and start the business with or without him. No matter what.

Reed sighed and pushed off the couch.

Why was he still thinking about it? He'd made his choice. A stack of reports to mark up this weekend towered on his counter. Life was back to normal.

But he didn't want normal. He wanted…

To start the business with Dale as his superintendent and Claire by his side every minute of every day. It would only take a minute to call her, to ask how she was doing. Were the otters okay? Did she get the zoo job? Would she forgive him?

He picked up the phone, dialed.

"Hello?"

"Barbara?" Reed had called Barbara the day after his heart-to-heart with Dad, and he'd apologized. Asked her if she'd forgive him. She'd been thrilled.

"Hi, Reed. Should I get your father?"

"No, actually, I wanted to ask you something. It's… well, I need some advice."

"I'll be happy to try."

"It's about Lake Endwell."

"Sure. What do you want to know?"

"I'm not sure I fit in there."

"What makes you think that?"

Reed swallowed. Opening up, revealing things, being vulnerable—this was just as hard as he'd expected. "I tend to leave casualties in my wake. Mom's family. Collin's."

"Reed." She had her stern voice on. "You listen to me and you listen good. Your mom's family lost *you*. Collin's family lost *you*. They chose to cut a worthy young man out of their lives, and the loss was all theirs. And for the record, your dad and I knew you were never to blame for Collin's mistakes."

Barbara had had every reason to write him off from day one. He'd never warmed to her. Never let her inside his world. And yet she'd seen beyond his hard shell to the person he was inside and…believed he wouldn't do drugs or blame his friend. His throat closed in.

When he didn't answer, she asked, "Does this have anything to do with Claire?"

"It might." He tightened his fingers around the phone. Was perspiration breaking out on his upper lip?

"I like Claire," she said.

So did he. A little too much. Was he an idiot for leaving her? She loved him. He loved her. Why was this so complicated?

"Yeah," he said. "Claire's special."

Barbara made a tsk-tsk sound. "But you're scared to take a chance?"

"Every time I get close to people, I lose them. I finally have Dad back, but will it last? The only person I haven't lost is Jake and only because I made sure to live far away from him."

"Reed, God wants you to have a full life. You might think you've protected Jake by staying away, but the only thing you've done is protect yourself from getting hurt."

"Maybe you're right. I've been praying." He'd been on his knees more times in the last week than in his entire life.

"Good. Praying is the best thing to do. Do you feel led one way or the other?"

"I was led to call you." A frustrated breath escaped. "What do I do?"

"Keep praying. And take a chance."

"Thanks."

"Anytime, Reed."

He hung up, his thoughts all over the place. His gaze landed on his worn Bible.

Lord, my head tells me I'm doing the right thing by staying here, but my heart says I'm making a mistake. Is Barbara right? Am I protecting myself? I don't know Your will. Show me what to do.

Opening the Bible, he flipped to the Psalms. The words practically jumped out at him.

He rubbed his eyes and read it again.

Boy, did they stand out!

"God sets the lonely in families, he leads forth the prisoners with singing; but the rebellious live in a sun-scorched land."

God sets the lonely in families...

He bowed his head, overcome with clarity. *You used my time in Lake Endwell to bring me to my family. Claire made it possible for me. You put me there. I was lonely.*

I am lonely.

And in that moment, he knew what he was going to do.

Claire surveyed her backyard, empty of toys, empty of otters. The babies had moved to the zoo yesterday. She'd said goodbye and cried all the way home.

Life had changed too much this summer.

She slipped out of the backyard and trekked next door. No Reed. Just a vacant cottage.

Like her vacant backyard.

And her vacant heart.

Claire sat on the edge of the dock with her feet in the water. The forest across the lake waved to her. She didn't wave back. Instead she squeezed her eyes shut, ignoring the whispers in her head, the voice of Aunt Sally asking if she was afraid to leave her family, the plea in Reed's eyes when he told her he had to go.

God, this isn't what I had planned.

What did she have planned? She'd known the otters couldn't stay. Known Reed couldn't either. But she never realized she'd be so desolate in the aftermath.

A sob choked her, and she tried to hold it back, but it erupted. Another followed, and another, until tears flooded her face, and she went beyond sobbing to the ugly cry with hiccups.

What was she supposed to do? Her life's purpose was here. Taking care of her family.

Wasn't it?

She sniffled, wiping her nose. Of course it was. Being here for Libby and everyone else fulfilled her. And she started her new position at the zoo next week.

But Libby had Jake to watch out for her now. And her brothers had each other. And the otters would be cared for no matter what.

Could her purpose have changed?

I've been clinging to something You only intended as temporary, haven't I?

A fish jumped two feet in front of her. The splash rippled out to her feet.

Was God taking away everything she loved?

Or had He taken away these things to get her on the path He'd planned for her all along?

She had the job. She could be with the otters. She had her family. She could see them every day.

But none of it was enough.

Because she only wanted one thing. And he lived in Chicago.

"Two more hours. I have a million things to do first." Claire raced around her bedroom, throwing tank tops, sundresses, sandals and anything else she touched onto her pastel pink-and-green-striped comforter. "Don't just stand there. Help me!"

Libby folded her arms over her chest. "What in the world are you doing?"

"I'm taking a risk."

"By getting rid of your entire wardrobe?"

"No, Libs, I'm going after Reed."

Libby perked up and fluttered over to the bed. "Going after Reed? Like how? What's your plan?"

Claire blew a piece of hair out of her eyes, held up a red dress and checked it with a critical eye. "If he can't live here, I'm moving. I'm not giving up on my chance at happiness."

Libby's mouth dropped open. "When did you decide to do this?"

"This morning. I've been miserable ever since he left."

"What about the job at the zoo? You've wanted to work there since...well, since you were in the womb. You would give that up?"

"Yep." Claire threw the dress on top of the pile. A good color on her, it would show off her tan. If she was confronting Reed, she needed every piece of ammo she could find.

"Okay, who are you and what have you done with my rational, responsible big sister?"

Claire cocked her head to the side. "I'm tired of being the rational, responsible big sister. I want to be reckless. Loved."

"But you are loved. We all love you. You can't leave!" Libby's pale blue eyes swam with sincerity.

"I don't know if Reed will even want me. But I have to try. I have to know I poured everything I could into this relationship. If it doesn't work out, at least I gave it my all."

"Why wouldn't he want you?" Libby let out a huffy

breath. "Any guy should be on his knees in gratitude that he could date you."

Claire crossed the room and hugged her. "Thank you. That's the sweetest thing I've heard in a long time."

Libby sniffed. "Well, it's true. Reed's the first guy I've met who is actually worth your time."

Claire grinned. "I agree."

"You're sure about this?"

"I am." God had sent her what she'd been too afraid to ask for. Reed. She belonged with him.

"Do you know where he is?" Libby picked up one of Claire's T-shirts and quickly tossed it back.

"No. That's why I needed you to come over. Can you call Jake and have him find out? I don't want Reed to know I'm coming. And for the love of all that's good in the world, do not tell Dad or our brothers!"

"I'm not an idiot, Claire." Libby pulled her cell phone out. "Wait, you can't go until after the grand reopening party tonight."

"I know." She swiped her hair off her forehead. "I'm going to the party for an hour. After that, I'm hitting the road."

"What if he's not in Chicago anymore? What if he's traveling for his job?"

"Then it will be a longer road trip than I anticipated. Will you call Jake already and get some addresses for me?"

"Maybe I should come with you." Libby tapped her phone against her palm. "If you get there and he's not interested..."

"He told me he loves me."

"Oh!"

Claire launched a black dress onto the pile. "I'm going to need another favor."

"What?" Libby pressed buttons on her phone.

"I need you to check on the otters for me while I'm gone."

"What? I don't do critters."

Claire scurried to the bathroom, where she riffled through her makeup. She tossed lipsticks, mascara and eyeliners into a cosmetic bag. "They aren't critters. They are sweet little furry babies. They love you. They always come running when you're here."

"They come running when anyone is here." Libby made a disgusted sound. "Fine. What do I have to do?"

"Go to the zoo while I'm gone and take pictures of them and send them to me on my phone so I know they're okay in their new quarters. I'll ask Tina to give you the clearance to get in."

Libby's lips curled down.

"For me, Libby? I'm worried to death about them. They moved yesterday and have to be quarantined for a month. What if they miss me?"

"Fine."

Winding the cord around her curling iron, Claire hustled back to her bed and studied the pile. Maybe she should go shopping. Buy a new outfit or ten.

"Okay, I've got the info." Libby held up a finger. "Reed is in Chicago. I'll write down the address for you."

Claire swept Libby into a hug and bounced. "Thank you, Libs! Maybe I should skip the restaurant and drive straight there."

"Go to the party for a little while. For Aunt Sally's sake."

"You're right."

"Want me to help you get ready?" Libby asked. "What are you going to wear?"

Claire surveyed the disaster in her room. "I have no idea."

Libby's lips twisted into a wicked grin. "I know exactly what you're going to wear."

She blinked and bit her lower lip. Libby had her determined tone on. The one that scared Claire to her core. But this was for Reed. And Libby had more style than anyone Claire knew.

Claire raised her hands. "Do what you have to do."

Chapter Nineteen

"There you are. Why haven't you called us? I must have left ten messages." Tommy, standing tall with his chest out and legs wide, blocked Claire's path.

Claire pushed past him. "I've been busy."

The new-and-improved restaurant had never looked better. The paneled walls had been polished, the mounted antlers dusted and rehung. It smelled like fish fry, a meal Claire dared not touch with her stomach so queasy. Lights from the chandeliers bounced off every surface, and the sound of laughter and conversation filled the air.

"Are you doing okay?" Tommy tilted his head to the side, his eyes full of concern.

She sighed. "It's been a rough couple of weeks."

"I know," Tommy said. "That's why I kept calling. I stopped by too, but you weren't home."

She adjusted the skirt of the plum halter dress Libby had insisted she wear tonight.

He brought his knuckle to his chin. "Is this about Reed?"

Heat flooded her neck and cheeks.

"Bryan and I—well, we overreacted." He shoved his hands in his pockets. "We've been talking with Sam and Dad, and we realized we needed to come up with a long-term plan for Sheffield Auto whether Reed moves here or not. We have it worked out. Since you and Libby are part owners, we wanted you to know what we came up with."

He filled her in on the basics. Claire caught her breath and met his gaze. "How does Dad feel about it?"

Tommy grinned and slung his arm over her shoulder. "He's happy. We're happy. And it will ensure that Sheffield Auto runs smoothly when Dad decides to retire."

"Does he want to retire?" They strolled to the back patio, where round tables held candles glowing in hurricane vases. Groups of people, drinks in hand, chatted and laughed. The whole town had turned out for the grand reopening. She'd enjoy it more if her stomach wasn't doing the tango.

"If we can convince Reed to move here, then, yeah, I'd say Dad wants out of the auto business."

"You want Reed here?" She halted. Maybe she should have taken a few of those brotherly calls.

"We've been harassing him all week."

Was Reed talking to her brothers but not her? It would crush her plan. How could she give up everything—her dream job, her family, her cottage—for a man who could discuss his life with her brothers but not her? "And what did he say?"

"Hasn't picked up his phone. Bryan and I had half a mind to hop in my truck and drive there the other night."

Her temples pounded—Reed hadn't been chatting with her brothers behind her back.

Tommy sat at an empty table. "Dad told us we were being selfish. He was right. Who are we to tell Reed to give up a big career to move here and start from scratch?"

Claire gazed out at the lake. Boats whizzed by in the direction of the sun. She hadn't confided in any of the men in her family—they would try to talk her out of her plan— but Tommy's honesty untied her tongue.

"I'm going after him, Tommy. Tonight."

"You're going to bring him back? Great idea!" He slapped his palm flat on the table and grinned at her. "He'll listen to you."

"No." She shook her head, the fabric of her dress swishing against her legs in the breeze. "I'm going to him."

Tommy frowned, small lines marring his handsome features. "What are you talking about?"

Serenity infused her. She smiled. "I love him. I'll move if I have to, but I'm not losing him." His cheekbones strained against his skin as his face grew red and his jaw jutted. Claire lifted her chin, ready to defend her choice. "Don't try to talk me out of it."

"Does Dad know?" His quiet words held danger.

She selected her reply with care. "Nobody knows except Libby. I want to keep it that way."

Tommy opened his mouth then shut it. "When?"

"Soon."

"How soon?"

"About ten minutes," she said. "I'm driving to his apartment tonight."

The muscle in his cheek jumped. "I don't like this. You're not spending the night with him."

"Of course not!" Claire refrained from rolling her eyes. "I booked a hotel."

"I'll go with you. It's not safe driving through a big city at night."

She inhaled, counting to three. Tommy meant well, but...

"Excuse me." A familiar voice came across the loudspeaker. "I need Claire Sheffield to the front at once. Claire Sheffield."

Claire met Tommy's stunned gaze. What in the world?

"Claire Sheffield. If you're here, come to the front."

Reed clutched the microphone on the small stage next to the bar. He searched the crowd, trying to catch a glimpse of Claire's dark hair, but a sea of faces watched him in expectation. His bad leg trembled, and he fought not to tap his hand against his other thigh. He hadn't eaten since lunch, which was a good thing, since his stomach seemed to be riding a tidal wave.

Should he call Claire to the stage one more time? Or should he face facts and admit she didn't want to see him? He had no doubt she was there—she wouldn't miss Sally and Joe's reopening.

Over by the back corner where two sets of doors led to the outdoor patio, a commotion stirred, parting the crowd in two.

Claire stepped inside. Reed released the breath he'd been holding. He drank her in—her shiny hair spilled over her shoulders, the dark purple dress that hugged her in all the right places, her pert nose, her eyes shocked. He drew his chest up and lifted the microphone again.

"Claire." Her name on his lips was a caress, a low invitation. "You're here.

She didn't move.

"Six weeks ago, I walked into this restaurant, and my life hasn't been the same since. I thought it was your eyes. Did you know you have a midnight-blue ring around each iris? They're the most unusual, beautiful eyes I've ever seen."

A low murmur rippled through the female part of the crowd.

"We rode out the tornado here," he continued. "My leg broke. And you stayed with me. Took care of me. Your family stopped by to help me with all the tasks I found impossible."

He couldn't take his gaze off her. His heart throbbed as her eyes grew round and filled with tears.

"You became my best friend," he said. "I haven't had

one of those in a long time. You still are. I haven't acted like one lately, and I'm sorry for that. You deserve better."

He kept the mic close, determined to make her understand how important she was to him—important enough for him to declare everything in front of her family and friends.

"I love you. I love that you made me see the truth about my past. I love that you keep otters in your backyard. I love your laid-back style, the way your head tips back when you laugh and your taste in movies. I love your zoo wardrobe. I love your family."

He broke eye contact with her to locate Dale and her brothers. Jake had his arm around Libby near the front door.

"Dale, you've been a mentor to me. Tommy, Bryan, Sam—you treat me like a brother. Libby—I'm honored you're going to be my sister soon."

Reed turned back to Claire. Tears streamed down her cheeks.

"Claire, I'm back. For good. I'm not interested in promotions or Chicago. The only thing I can think about is you."

He set the mic back on its stand and loped down the two steps to the floor. Everyone parted for him. He stopped in front of Claire.

"Forgive me?"

Claire laughed, swabbing under her eyes with the backs of her hands. Then she dragged him to the back doors, outside over the patio to the deck leading out to the lake. When they reached the edge, she whirled and threw herself into his arms, burying her face in his shoulder.

He held her tightly, lowering his head next to hers. She breathed in his cologne, savored his hard muscles, his warmth, his tender kiss on her hair. She couldn't believe it—couldn't believe he'd come back. And said all that. In front of everyone!

"Reed. You...I can't believe it. What you said—I'm—" She stared in his eyes, and the love she witnessed triggered her tears again.

"Hey, don't cry," he said, running his hands up and down her arms. "I didn't want to upset you. Please stop crying."

"You didn't upset me." She hiccupped in an attempt to laugh. "You made me the happiest woman in the world. I can't believe it. I was two minutes away from driving to Chicago to be with you."

His eyes darkened, and two lines creased his forehead. "What are you talking about?"

"I made up my mind this morning. Living here isn't the same without you. I figured I could start over wherever you were."

He exhaled, straightened, rubbing his hand over the back of his neck. "You would do that?"

She nodded.

"Why?"

"Because I love you." She shoved his shoulder and smiled. "I told you that."

"But what about the zoo and the otters and your cottage and your family?"

"They still aren't you."

Questions lingered in his expression. She cupped his cheeks with her hands. "You're more important. Everything you said just now—I know. I feel it too. The last six weeks changed me. I thought I had enough before you showed up. I was content. But God sent you here. I felt like He was asking me if I wanted more. And I realized I did. I had to come to grips with prioritizing my life."

"I could never ask you to move for me."

"But I asked you to move for me," she said. "How could I not do the same for you?"

He hauled her to him, wrapped his hands around her waist and claimed her lips with his. She softened under his touch, drinking in his love. Her knees weakened and she murmured as he drew her closer.

An odd clamor broke them apart.

"What in the—" Reed turned to see the commotion.

The restaurant had emptied, and everyone stood on the lawn cheering, hooting and whistling.

Claire closed her eyes. She'd have to throw herself in the lake. She would never, ever live this down. But Reed kept her next to him and waved to everyone. The big grin on his face was contagious, and rather than squirm out of his arms and dive into the water, she leaned her head on his shoulder.

"I will get you back for this," she whispered.

"For what? Kissing you again?" He shifted, leaning in to kiss her, but she jerked her face away, shaking her head as her mouth grew into a wide smile.

"You are done embarrassing me in public, mister."

"Sorry, Claire, but I'm not done yet."

This time he did kiss her. She couldn't do anything about it.

And she didn't want to.

Epilogue

Fat flakes of snow swirled outside the windows. Claire moved the ladder near the entrance of Uncle Joe's Restaurant, then swiped a dozen balloons. Christmas had come and gone without event, and the new year would be upon them next week. She'd been a teeny bit disappointed Reed hadn't proposed at Christmas, but how could she complain when he always put her first in his life?

"Feels familiar, doesn't it, hon? We're old pros." Aunt Sally whizzed by, her hands full of candles on her way to the head table. "This time, though, the wedding will happen. Rain, shine, tornado, hurricane, snowstorm—I don't care. Libby and Jake will have their wedding."

Claire laughed, climbing two rungs. "We should be okay. No blizzards in the forecast, thankfully." She counted out six pink and six silver ribbons, tore a piece of tape off and moved up another rung.

"Anybody showing up at the zoo now that it's gotten cold?"

"Not too many during the day. Only for the light show at night. Hansel and Gretel are loving this weather, though. You should see them."

"I'll have to stop by soon." Aunt Sally finished setting the candleholders out. "Your dad told me he and Reed bought the farmland on Bates Highway. I take it they're going to develop it now the stores downtown are almost finished?"

"Yeah. They're putting in a new subdivision. The roads will be cut in before the town celebration on Memorial Day."

Sally adjusted tablecloths and candles on her way back to Claire. "We're blessed he came when he did. Just what this town needed."

Claire agreed. After moving to Lake Endwell in July, Reed had surprised her with his plans of rejuvenating a handful of run-down buildings outside town. He said businesses would be more likely to stay and prosper. Reed never ran out of ideas, and Dad never ran out of energy—they were the perfect pair to be in business together.

"Did Reed get all his stuff moved out of Jake's apartment?" Aunt Sally put the final decorations on the gift table.

"Yep. As of Christmas night, he's back to living in Granddad's cottage."

Aunt Sally smiled. "Well, Libby will be glad. I don't think she wanted to have an extra roommate."

Claire stretched on her tiptoes to hang the balloons and chuckled. "No, she wouldn't. Reed almost moved in with Tommy and Bryan, but we told him it was crazy. He belongs in the cottage."

"Let's see. Is there anything else I can do? I want to get back and finish decorating the cake."

Claire stepped off the ladder and hugged Aunt Sally. "Go on home. Reed will be here any minute."

"I can wait," Sally said.

"If Reed says he'll do something, he does it. Don't worry."

"You call me if you need me." She grabbed her coat and purse, waved and left.

Claire gathered her final bunch of balloons and made it up two steps when the door opened with a whoosh.

"Brrr...it's cold out there." Reed closed the door and shook the snow off his wool coat.

Whoa! That man could ignite a forest fire in the dead of winter.

"Hey, beautiful." Shrugging his coat off, he draped it over the back of a chair. "This looks great."

"Thanks." She climbed down, giving him a light kiss. "But you can put your coat back on. After this bunch, I'm done."

"Wait." He put his hands around her waist, his eyes glowing with intensity. "Do you know it's been almost seven months since we met?"

She wriggled her arms around his neck and smiled. "Really?"

"Uh-huh. And since it's kind of our anniversary, I have something for you."

"Oh, yeah?" Claire asked. "A gift for a kind-of anniversary?"

"Yeah." He lowered himself to one knee.

Her mind floundered. Could he be...? No. He wasn't proposing. Was he?

Her heartbeat accelerated, thumping faster than she thought possible.

"Claire, you know I love you." He reached into his pocket and pulled out a box from JoJo's Jewelry. "I want to spend every minute with you for the rest of my life. Tornadoes, hurricanes, earthquakes—I'll weather any of it at your side. What do you say—will you make me the happiest man on earth? Will you marry me?"

She dropped to her knees, hugging him, kissing him. "Yes, oh, yes!"

Slowly, he rose, helping her to her feet and taking her

left hand in his. He pulled out a diamond ring and slid it on her finger. "You're sure?"

"I've never been so sure of anything in my life."

He kissed her. Thoroughly.

"You amaze me." Claire admired the ring, twisting her hand this way and that, loving the way it sparkled.

"Do I otterly amaze you?" His teasing smile made her grin, and she burst out laughing.

"Otterly."

* * * * *

Dear Reader,

When I was growing up in mid-Michigan, we spent many weekends up north at my grandparents' rustic cabin. I always wondered what it would be like to live in one of the pretty cottages on the lake. Writing about fictional Lake Endwell let me fulfill that daydream. Isn't it delightful to open a book and enter a different world? My stories are usually set in small towns and feature children or animals. Several years ago, a church member who worked at the zoo brought an otter home for a few days because the little guy wasn't acclimating to his surroundings. His antics inspired me to have Claire foster the otter twins.

Family also plays a big role in this book. Have you read Psalm 68:6a? "God sets the lonely in families, He leads forth the prisoners with singing." It took a tornado and a broken leg for Reed to stay in Lake Endwell, but God used both to bless him with a family. If you're facing difficulties, keep praying. Your blessing could be right around the corner. I love hearing from you. Please stop by my website, www.jillkemerer.com, and email me at jill@jillkemerer.com.

God bless you!

Jill Kemerer

COMING NEXT MONTH FROM
Love Inspired®

Available April 21, 2015

THE RANCHER TAKES A BRIDE
Martin's Crossing • by Brenda Minton
When Oregon Jeffries introduces rancher Duke Martin to the daughter he never knew he had, can they move beyond the mistakes of their pasts and build a future together?

THE DOCTOR'S SECOND CHANCE
by Missy Tippens
Having given up her child for adoption years ago, Dr. Violet Remy is given a second chance at the family she's always longed for when new daddy Jake West seeks her help in raising his adorable baby niece.

THE SINGLE DAD FINDS A WIFE
Cedar Springs • by Felicia Mason
Dr. Spring Darling wants a family of her own. But when she falls for single dad David Camden and his little boy, can she get past the architect's plan to ruin her historic family home?

WINNING THE TEACHER'S HEART
The Donnelly Brothers • by Jean C. Gordon
Single mom Becca Norton is fighting Jared Donnelly for the preservation of her neighborhood, yet when she must battle for custody of her children, can this former bad boy come to her family's rescue?

BACHELOR TO THE RESCUE
Home to Dover • by Lorraine Beatty
Connected by a mutual tragedy, Shawn McKinney promises to care for widow Lainie Hollings and her girls. Can working together to restore the town library bridge the gap between these two wounded hearts?

A FIREFIGHTER'S PROMISE
by Patricia Johns
Firefighter Matt Bailey needs a fresh start in a new town. But he can't abandon the boy he once found on his doorstep—or the boy's amazing adoptive mom. Despite his past mistakes, can he be the hero they both need?

LOOK FOR THESE AND OTHER LOVE INSPIRED BOOKS WHEREVER BOOKS ARE SOLD, INCLUDING MOST BOOKSTORES, SUPERMARKETS, DISCOUNT STORES AND DRUGSTORES.

LICNM0415

JUST CAN'T GET ENOUGH OF INSPIRATIONAL ROMANCE?

Join our social communities
and talk to us online!
You will have access to the latest
news on upcoming titles and special
promotions, but most important,
you can talk to other fans about your
favorite Love Inspired® reads.

 www.Facebook.com/LoveInspiredBooks

 www.Twitter.com/LoveInspiredBks

Harlequin.com/Community

LISOCIAL